CALUMET
COPPER
CREATURES

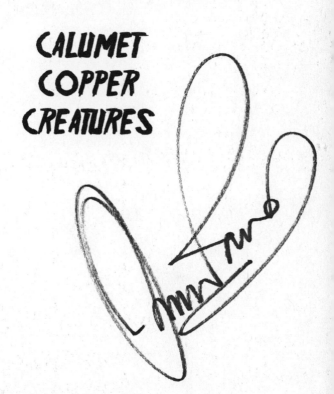

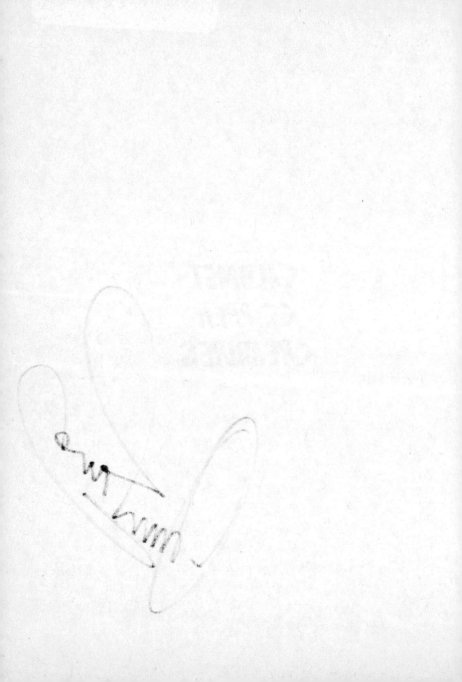

Here's what readers from around the country are saying about Johnathan Rand's AMERICAN CHILLERS:

"MISSISSIPPI MEGALODON was awesome! You're the best writer in the WORLD!"

-Julian T., age 8, Florida

"American Chillers is the best book series in the world! I love them!"

-Anneliese B., age 10, Michigan

"I'm reading FLORIDA FOG PHANTOMS, and it's great! When are you going to write a book about Utah?"

-David H., Age 7, Utah

"MISSISSIPPI MEGALODON is so rad! Where in the world do you get these ideas? You are the awesomest author ever!"

-Eli L., Age 9, Illinois

"I read DANGEROUS DOLLS OF DELAWARE and it was super creepy. My favorite book is POLTERGEISTS OF PETOSKEY. You make me like to read even more!"

-Brendon P., Age 8, Michigan

"I love your books! I just finished SINISTER SPIDERS OF SAGINAW. It really freaked me out! Now I'm reading MIS-SISSIPPI MEGALODON. It's really good. Can you come to our school?"

-Blane B., age 11, Indiana

"I'm your biggest fan in the world! I just started your DOUBLE THRILLERS and it's great!"

-Curtis J., Age 11, California

"I just read the book: CURSE OF THE CONNECTICUT COYOTES and it really freaked me out when Erica thought she got attacked by a coyote!"

-Shaina B., Age 10, Minnesota

"I love your books so much that I read everyone in my school library and public library! I hope I get a chance to come to CHILLERMANIA, and I'm saving my money to make it happen. You rock! Keep writing, and I'm your biggest fan!"

-Makayla B., Age 9, Missouri

"Your books are the best I've ever read in my life! I've read over 20 and double thumbs up to all of them!"

-Justus K., Age 11, California

"I never like to read until I discovered your books. The first one I read was VIRTUAL VAMPIRES OF VERMONT, and it totally freaked me out! Me and my friends have our own American Chillers book club. Will you come to one of our meetings?"

-Carson C., age 12, Oklahoma

"I love the American Chillers series I only have three more books to go! My favorite book is HAUNTING IN NEW HAMPSHIRE. It's awesome!"

-Eriana S., age 10, Ohio

"I've read most of your American Chillers books! My favorite was WISCONSIN WEREWOLVES. Right now I am reading KENTUCKY KOMODO DRAGONS. I love it because it is mystery/adventure/chillers! Thank you for writing such exciting books!"

-Maya R., age 9, Georgia

"When we visited my grandparents in San Diego, I found your books at *The Yellow Book Road* bookstore. I bought one and read it in three days! My grandparents took me back to the bookstore and bought me five more! I can't stop reading them!"

-Amber Y, age 11, Hawaii

"I've read every single one of your Michigan and American Chillers and they're all great! I just finished VICIOUS VACUUMS OF VIRGINIA and I think it's the best one yet! Go Johnathan Rand!"

-Avery R., age 10, Delaware

"Your books are the best ones I've ever read! I tried to write my own, but it's hard! How do you come up with so many great books? Please tell me so I can be a writer, too!"

-Lauren H., age 12, Montana

"My family and I were vacationing in northern Michigan and stopped at CHILLERMANIA and you were there! It was the best day of my life!"

-Andrew T., age 8, Tennessee

Got something cool to say about Johnathan Rand's books? Let us know, and we might publish it right here! Send your short blurb to:

**Chiller Blurbs
281 Cool Blurbs Ave.
Topinabee, MI 49791**

Other books by Johnathan Rand:

#15: Calumet Copper Creatures

Johnathan Rand

An AudioCraft Publishing, Inc. book

This book is a work of fiction. Names, places, characters and incidents are used fictitiously, or are products of the author's very active imagination.

Book storage and warehouses provided by Chillermania!©
Indian River, Michigan

Michigan Chillers #15: Calumet Copper Creatures
ISBN 13-digit: 978-1-893699-66-3

Librarians/Media Specialists:
PCIP/MARC records available **free of charge** at
www.americanchillers.com

Cover illustration by Dwayne Harris
Cover layout and design by Sue Harring

Printed in USA

CALUMET
COPPER
CREATURES

VISIT CHILLERMANIA!

WORLD HEADQUARTERS FOR BOOKS BY JOHNATHAN RAND!

Yooperland

Indian River

Alpena

Traverse City

MICHIGAN

CHILLERMANIA!

**I-75 Exit 313
then south
1 mile!**

Mt. Pleasant

Bay City

Grand Rapids

Lansing

Detroit

Kalamazoo

Visit the HOME for books by Johnathan Rand! Featuring books, hats, shirts, bookmarks and other cool stuff not available anywhere else in the world! Plus, watch the American Chillers website for news of special events and signings at *CHILLERMANIA!* with author Johnathan Rand! Located in northern lower Michigan, on I-75! Take exit 313 . . . then south 1 mile! For more info, call (231) 238-0338. And be afraid! Be veeeery afraaaaaaiiiid . . . .

1

"Mom, have you seen my hiking shoes?" my brother called out. He'd been looking for them for ten minutes, and he still hadn't found them.

"Have you checked the garage, Calvin?" Mom asked. She was in the living room, putting on her sweater, getting ready to go shopping in town.

"I'll look again," Calvin said as he strode through the kitchen and through the side door that led to the garage.

"Mikayla," Mom said to me, "you keep an eye on your brother while I'm gone. Don't let him get into trouble like last week."

I rolled my eyes. "Yes, Mom," I said.

Last week while Mom had been on her weekly shopping trip, Calvin was hitting rocks with an old tennis racquet. One of the rocks broke a window in a house across the street. Oh, it was an accident. Calvin didn't mean to do it. But the window was still broken. Calvin didn't have enough money to pay for it, so Mom had to. Calvin was paying Mom back over the summer by doing odd jobs around the house.

And I got into a little trouble, too. I'm eleven, and Calvin is eight. I was supposed to be watching him, but I had been on the phone, talking to a friend. I knew what Calvin was doing, because I could see him in the yard, swinging the racquet at stones he was tossing into the air . . . but I never thought he might actually break a window.

Mom left to go shopping in town. We live in Calumet, which is a city in Michigan's Upper Peninsula. It's a great place to live, but you'd better like snow. We get a *ton* of it in the winter! Sometimes, we get so much snow that the city streets look like tunnels after they've been plowed.

And summers are great. Calumet is small, compared to some of Michigan's larger cities, and it's surrounded by lots of woods. Plus, Lake Superior is only a few miles away. There are many smaller lakes around, too. Sometimes, my brother and I go fishing or swimming in them.

But Calumet used to be known for something else: copper. Years ago, Calumet was a big copper mining town, and one company ran all of the mines. It's hard to believe that in 1900 there were over 20,000 people living in the area. Today, there are only about 1,000. And to this day, 2,000 miles of copper mines snake beneath the village and all around. Most of the mines went out of business during the Great Depression, and the rest were shut down by a labor strike in 1968.

At least, that's what everyone was *told*.

Problem is, that wasn't the truth. The mines were actually closed because of mysterious copper creatures. They thought if they closed the mines and sealed them up, the creatures would never surface again.

And they were right—for a while, the creatures didn't return. Very few people even knew about them. The copper creatures kept to themselves, deep in the mines, never seen by anyone.

Until this summer.

This summer the copper creatures came out of hiding, and two very unfortunate kids in Calumet were going to discover them:

Calvin and me.

2

Calvin returned from the garage with his hiking shoes. He'd finally found them.

"Let's go exploring," he said. Calvin has been on this kick to go 'exploring' in the woods. He likes to hike down the trail and then go off on his own to see what he can find.

Trouble is, being that he's only eight, he can't go alone. So, Mom usually makes me go with him. Sometimes it's fun, but other times, it's just plain boring. We never find much of anything. Oh, we see lots of animals: deer, raccoons, snakes, birds, toads . . . things like that. But we never really find anything exciting. Once, Calvin found the skull of a deer. He took it home, cleaned it up, and put it on his dresser. It's still there. Gross.

And today, I wasn't really interested in going for a hike. But two things changed my mind: one, I really couldn't think of anything better to do, and two, I knew that if I took Calvin exploring, he wouldn't get into trouble . . . which meant *I* wouldn't get into trouble.

"Where do you want to go?" I asked.

Calvin shrugged. "I don't care," he replied. "Anywhere different. Let's go somewhere we haven't been before."

"We could ride our bikes over to St. Louis Mine Road and find a trail that goes off into the woods," I suggested.

"Hey, that would be cool!" Calvin said. "That'll be the perfect place to do some exploring!"

It's also the perfect place to keep you from

breaking any more windows, I thought.

St. Louis Mine Road runs east of town, and there are woods and fields on both sides. I've been out there many times before, but not Calvin. This would be a new place for him to explore, so I knew he'd be excited.

In no time at all, we put on our helmets, hopped onto our bikes, and were pedaling down the block, rounding onto 1st Street, which becomes St. Louis Mine Road.

"I wonder what we'll find," Calvin said as we pedaled beneath the gray, overcast sky.

"You never know," I said.

We continued riding on the shoulder of the road. Calvin kept his eye out for anything he thought might be worth exploring.

Suddenly, he hit his brakes hard. Gravel crunched as his bike came to a halt. I stopped and turned around to look at him.

"What's the matter?" I asked.

Calvin was looking into the woods, and he raised his arm to point.

"I saw something over there," he said.

"What did you see?" I asked.

"I don't know," he said. "But something moved."

"It was probably just a deer," I replied.

"No, it wasn't a deer," Calvin said, shaking his head.

I stared for a moment, but all I could see were trees.

"Well, whatever it was, it's gone now," I said. "Come on . . . let's keep going."

"No," Calvin insisted. "Let's go see what it is."

I wasn't in the mood to argue, so I hopped off my bike. Calvin did the same. We took our helmets off and dropped them by our bikes. Then, we waded into the brush that encroached the shoulder of the road.

"It was right over there," Calvin said, pointing once again. "Let's go find out what kind of animal it was."

Well, we found it, all right. And it certainly

wasn't a deer. In fact, when we found out what it really was, I wished we'd never decided to go looking in the first place. Once again, Calvin had managed to get himself—and *me*—into trouble.

3

The brush was thick as we walked through the forest. Also: blackflies were trying to eat us alive. They're tiny, biting flies that suck all of your blood. Well, not *all* of it, of course, but it seems like it. When those little buggers bite, they hurt. They were swarming all around us, landing on my neck and arms.

"Where is this thing?" I asked with dismay. I was beginning to doubt that Calvin saw anything at all. Like I said: it was probably just a deer or something. So far, though, I hadn't seen a thing. Not even a tiny bird.

"I saw something move right around here somewhere," Calvin said, looking all around. "It has to be some sort of animal."

"Whatever it was, it's long gone," I said.

"No, it's not," Calvin insisted. "I would've seen it."

We moved slowly through the brush. The swarm of blackflies around my head was like a cloud, and I kept swatting my arm at them to keep them from landing and biting me. Calvin was doing the same thing.

Next time I'll remember bug spray, I thought.

"It was right around here where I saw it move," Calvin said. "But it might be gone by now."

I guess if there was one good thing, Calvin was occupied . . . and he wasn't doing anything to get into trouble by hunting for some animal in the woods.

Unfortunately, trouble of a different kind

was only moments away.

"I'm going to wait right here," I said, swishing the air to keep the blackflies away. "Let me know if you find something."

Oh, Calvin found something all right. No sooner had I spoken those words than something emerged from a brush pile. It emerged by standing on its hind legs and facing us.

And that something was a huge black bear!

Now, I don't know where you live, but where *we* live, we see black bears often. Oh, it's not like they wander into your yard or anything . . . although that does happen once in a while. Bears usually keep to themselves . . . like this one had been doing.

But now the bear was standing on his hind legs, which meant that he felt threatened. When a bear feels threatened, watch out. You never know what he'll do.

However, Calvin did the right thing: he yelled and clapped his hands, making lots of noise. The bear decided he didn't like the noise, dropped to all fours, and took off in the opposite direction, crashing through thick branches.

My heart was pounding. Bugs still swarmed my head, and I swatted at them.

"See?" Calvin said. "I told you I saw something!"

"Next time, let's get a better look before we go trudging into the woods," I said. "It's a good thing we didn't surprise that bear any more than we did. Otherwise, we might not have been so lucky."

"But that was cool, don't you think?" Calvin asked.

"Yes," I said, "it was cool. I just hope it doesn't happen again."

When we reached the shoulder of the road, we put our helmets back on, climbed back onto our bikes, and continued our journey. There was a thin, two-track trail I had seen before on an earlier ride. I'd heard that it was supposed to go way back into the woods, to an old ghost town or abandoned mining operation. There wasn't supposed to be anything there anymore, except old foundations and a few rotting structures that were falling down, but it would be neat to see. And Calvin would have a riot poking around and exploring.

We pedaled until we saw the trail I was looking for. It went off to the left, to the north, and it was heavily overgrown with tall grass.

"Let's go that way," I said.

"Where does it go?" Calvin asked as we slowed our bikes. We checked to make sure there were no cars coming, then we crossed the road.

"A ghost town," I replied.

"Awesome!" Calvin shouted. "Really?"

"That's what I hear," I said. "It's supposed to go to some town where miners used to live with their families. Years ago, when mines began shutting down, it was abandoned. Everybody moved away, and it turned into a ghost town."

"I've never been to a real ghost town before!" Calvin said as we rode our bikes off the shoulder and merged onto the two-track.

"Neither have I," I said. "I bet it will be cool-looking, if we can find it."

And we would. We weren't going to have any trouble at all finding the old ghost town. We would walk among the ruins; we would explore what was left of some very old buildings. We would even find an old penny with an Indian head on it.

But there was something else we would find.

Monsters.

Not monsters like you see on television or in comic books, not monsters made up for movies or stories.

Real monsters.

Creatures that lived in the abandoned copper mines, all these years, waiting for the right time to emerge, waiting for just the right opportunity.

The time had come.

The copper creatures were coming back.

And for Calvin and me, it was the beginning of what was to be the scariest day of our lives.

5

The old two-track was difficult to follow, because it was heavily overgrown with clumps of tall weeds and grass. Not only that: over the years, trees had fallen and hadn't been cleared away. The grass hid these trees from our view, so we had to be very careful not to hit them with our bicycles. Which meant that we had to go slowly. When we encountered one of these logs, we had to hop off our bikes and climb over it.

We rode deeper and deeper into the forest. I wasn't worried about getting lost, because the trail was easy to follow. I was more worried about the hundreds of blackflies that swarmed behind us. When we stopped, they buzzed erratically around our heads. Often, one would land on my neck or my face, and I had to smack it or sweep it away.

Calvin rode ahead of me. He was alert and excited about finding a ghost town.

"Where is this thing supposed to be?" he asked.

"It can't be much farther," I replied. "At least, not according to what I was told."

We continued weaving our way through the long grass, and my thoughts drifted back in time to the days when the miners and their families lived in the Calumet area. Back in the very early days, they didn't have modern conveniences that we have today. They didn't have indoor plumbing, electricity, or motorized vehicles. When they were hungry, they couldn't simply run down to the corner convenience store and get a bag of potato chips. I'm not sure I would have enjoyed living that lifestyle, but I still found it very fascinating.

Suddenly, Calvin stopped. He pointed.

"Look," he said.

I pulled up alongside of him and stopped.

Ahead of us, a wide field opened up, displaying the bony remains of what at one time had been a small community, probably built to house miners and their families many, many years ago. However, there wasn't much to see at all. All of the structures had fallen in on themselves. They'd been there for so long that trees grew right through the middle of what once had been a living room or bedroom. There wasn't much left standing, and even foundations made of stone and mortar had crumbled away to almost nothing.

I was a little disappointed. The only ghost towns I was familiar with were the ones I'd seen in books: ghost towns from the old West. In some of the old black and white pictures I'd seen, entire villages stood empty and vacant, as if everyone in town packed up everything one day and left.

That might have happened here, in the village we were looking at, but it had been so long ago that there really wasn't much of anything to see.

Still, Calvin was intensely fascinated. He sat on his bicycle seat, leaning forward on his handlebars, slowly turning his head as his eyes gazed across the remains of the structures in the field.

"I can't believe people used to live here," he said.

"It was a long time ago, that's for sure," I said. "No one's been here for decades. I'll bet we're the first people to be here in years."

"Let's go check it out," Calvin said as he slipped off his bicycle and laid it in the grass. I did the same. We both took off our helmets and placed them on our bikes.

Wind shook the trees. Limbs, branches, and leaves shuddered in the breeze. High above, a hawk soared beneath the cloudy, bone-colored sky.

Calvin began to walk through the tall grass,

but I didn't follow him. I was suddenly struck with a strange feeling, like a warning. It was as if there was a warning in the wind, a warning in the trembling leaves. Something seemed to be telling me to leave, to get my brother, turn around, and head home.

You're just being silly, Mikayla, I thought. *Trees can't talk. Wind doesn't talk. It's only your imagination, your own voice in your own head.*

I ignored the strange feeling and pushed those thoughts away as I began making my way through the tall grass, following Calvin into the ghost town.

Looking back at it now, I realized that if only I hadn't thought that it was silly, if only I would have listened to that voice in my head, if we would have turned around and went home, then nothing bad would've happened.

Of course, it's easy to think that now. When you look back at things, it's easy to see where you went wrong . . . and going to the ghost town was going to be a big, big mistake.

6

I rushed to catch up to Calvin, and we waded through the overgrown grass and brush. When we reached the remains of a house, we stopped.

"It doesn't look like much of anything," Calvin said.

"Well," I said, "nobody's been here for years. Everybody left, and there was nobody here to take care of anything. That's why they call it a ghost town. There's nothing left here but the abandoned buildings."

"And the ghosts," Calvin said. "Maybe we'll see one."

"Probably not," I said. "Ghosts only come out at night."

I had no idea if this was true or not, but it just seemed likely. Whenever I watched a ghost story on television, they came out only at night.

The foundations of the house we were looking at were really nothing but scattered rocks with the remains of a few rotting beams. Again, I was a little disappointed. I was hoping to find actual, standing homes and buildings. Nothing in this ghost town resembled anything like that.

"What we need," I said, "is to have a metal detector. I'll bet we could find some really cool stuff."

Calvin kneeled down next to a basketball-sized rock and rolled it over. He did this with several more rocks, and then stood.

"Let's check out a few other places," he said, and I followed him as he walked through the remains of the structure and out the other side. All the while, I tried to imagine what life had been like all those years ago. I tried to imagine what the homes and buildings looked like, where the main road was. It was so overgrown that it was impossible to know.

One good thing: the wind had picked up, and it kept the blackflies away. I didn't have to constantly smack at them on my neck or cheek.

"Wait a second," I said, and I stopped.

Calvin turned to me.

"What's up?" he asked.

"I think we must be in the middle of the village," I said. "I think this is the center of town."

We looked around. The trees trembled and shook in the wind. The tall grass swayed and bent.

Once again, I was struck by that strange feeling. A warning of some sort, something telling me to be careful, that danger was lurking nearby.

And once again, I pushed it away. I refused to let my imagination freak me out.

"Let's go over there," Calvin said, pointing.

"That looks like it used to be a huge building. Maybe we'll find something."

Oh, we were about to find something, all right. In less than sixty seconds, we were about to find ourselves in a lot of trouble.

7

Calvin took the lead, making his way through the dense grass. I was surprised at how tall it was. Some of the blades reached all the way up to my waist. We both had to be careful to watch where we were going, so we didn't trip over any rocks, stumps, or logs. We also needed to be careful not to step on anything more dangerous, like a rusty nail. Last summer, a friend of mine accidentally stepped on one of those and had to go to the hospital.

"It would be cool to find the entrance to one of the mines," Calvin said.

"They're all sealed off," I said. "And even if we found one that wasn't closed up, we couldn't go inside. It would be too dangerous."

"I didn't say we'd go inside," Calvin said. "I just said it would be cool to *find* one."

I followed Calvin until he stopped at the remains of what must've been the largest building in the village. However, there was no way of telling what it was. It could've been a big home, it could've been a grocery store or a mill of some sort. There was really nothing to see but the crumbling foundations and dark, rotting beams.

"Some ghost town this place is," Calvin said. "There's not much here at all."

At my feet, something small, dark, and round caught my attention. I knelt down and picked it up, amazed to find that it was an old, Indian head penny!

"Check this out!" I said, holding the worn

penny in the palm of my hand. Calvin turned and looked.

"Wow!" he said. "Where did you find that?"

I pointed at my feet. "Right there!"

I stuffed the penny safely into my front pocket, and we knelt down. For the next ten minutes, we searched the ground for more coins, but we found nothing.

"We need to come back with a metal detector," I said. "I'll bet we'd find all sorts of coins if we had one of those."

Finally, we gave up the search and stood. On the other side of the foundation, there appeared to be a brown can of some sort laying next to a large rock.

I pointed. "What's that?" I asked.

Calvin looked at where I was pointing. Then, he stepped over some rocks. I followed him as we walked through the remains of what was left of the large structure, over rocks and around rotting logs and wood. As we came closer to the object, it became clear what it was: an old, rusting lantern.

Calvin picked up the lantern by the handle. It was dented and the glass was broken out, but it most certainly was a lantern.

"Imagine having to use that instead of flipping a light switch," I said.

"Or a flashlight," Calvin said. "But it still looks cool. I'm going to take it home and put it in my room."

"Maybe it belongs to a ghost," I said. "Maybe a ghost picks it up at night and walks around, haunting this place."

Calvin rolled his eyes. "Right," he said. Then, he stepped over the rocks and into the grass. I followed.

"Hey," he said. "What's that over there?"

Ahead of us, only a few feet away, was a place in the field where no grass grew. It seemed very strange, being that everywhere else we looked, tall grass and weeds grew as thick as carpeting. But there was a space in front of us, about the size of a car, where there was no grass.

We walked toward it and stopped.

Nothing could grow in the space, because there was a hole in the ground. It had been carefully covered by slats of wood that were gray and old and weathered. Some of the boards had rotted away, exposing the darkness below.

"Looks like you got your wish," I said. "This looks like the entrance to a mine or a well."

"Wow," Calvin said. "I wonder how deep it goes."

"I have no idea," I said. "But there are miles and miles of mines beneath the ground. Then again, it could just be an old well. A long time ago, somebody boarded it up so nobody would fall in."

"I don't think those boards would hold anybody," Calvin said. He pointed. "Those things are all rotted and falling apart. If we walked on that thing, it would never hold our weight."

One thing we didn't realize, however, was that over the years, the ground around the hole had also slowly weathered away, making it soft and loose.

And *dangerous.*

Without any warning at all, the earth beneath our feet gave way. This caused all of the boards to collapse, and suddenly, we were falling, falling, both of us screaming, tumbling through the air with rotting boards and pieces of earth and rock twirling around us, falling, falling . . . .

8

Our fall was abruptly stopped, but pieces of wood continued to land around us. Then, everything was quiet. Something poked my ribs, but other than that, I was okay.

"Calvin?" I said. "Where are you? Are you okay?"

"You're on top of me," he grunted. "Get off me."

It was hard to see, because I was covered

with so much debris, but light streamed down from the wide opening above. We'd fallen about twenty feet, and we had been very, very lucky. Normally, a fall from that height would've meant broken bones, or worse. But we landed on some old boards that helped break our fall.

I pushed some of the slats away and stood. Then, I helped Calvin to his feet.

"Are you okay?" I asked again.

"Yeah," he said. "I think so. But how are we going to get out of here?"

We looked up. The sides of the hole had been firmed up with several large, vertical beams. It appeared that, at one time, there had been slats of wood nailed to the beams, creating a ladder of sorts. But most of those slats had rotted away, eliminating its use.

Fear welled up inside of me, and I remembered that strange feeling, that odd warning I felt upon arriving at the old ghost town.

We're in trouble now, I thought. *We have no way out of this mine shaft, or whatever it is, and nobody knows we're here.*

Calvin realized this at the same time.

"Mikayla," he said quietly. *"We're in a lot of trouble."*

I remembered the time that Calvin accidentally broke a window with a rock, and how I had been scolded, too. That was nothing compared to the trouble we were in now. Now, I really wasn't worried about getting scolded. I was worried about getting out of the mine shaft alive.

Calvin fumbled around in the darkness, and suddenly, a light clicked on. A round, white circle the size of a beach ball illuminated the sides of the mine shaft.

"Where did you get a flashlight?" I asked.

"I brought it from home," Calvin said. "It's just one of those tiny ones with a key ring." He held it out. Sure enough, it was a small flashlight, about half the size of a pencil. "Mom gave it to me. When you told me we were going to go exploring, I wanted to make sure we were prepared."

"Prepared for what?" I asked.

"I don't know," he replied. "Anything. You never know what you're going to need when you go exploring."

While I thought it was silly to pack a flashlight when we'd be exploring during the day, I sure was glad he did. We might not be able to get out of the mine shaft, but at least we could see. It wasn't much comfort, but it helped a little . . . until Calvin shined the light behind us, and we saw the long, dark tunnel—a mine shaft—stretching deep into the earth like a gaping, black mouth.

9

The tiny light Calvin brought wasn't powerful enough to illuminate the entire tunnel. The heavy blackness seemed to eat the beam, and it was impossible to see more than a few feet in front of us.

"Where do you think that leads to?" Calvin asked as we peered into the inky blackness of the mine shaft.

"I have no idea," I replied.

"Do you think we should follow it?" Calvin asked.

I wasn't sure. But, then again, we really didn't have any other options. It was impossible to climb straight up, so the only place we could go was through the mine.

But there was a problem with that, too. The mines beneath the town of Calumet went for miles and miles and miles. We would have no way of knowing where to go, where to turn, or how to get out. In the mines, it would be easy to get lost, running into dead end after dead end after dead end.

So, that was our dilemma: if we stayed where we were and waited for someone to find us, we could wait for days. We could yell and shout and scream, but no one would hear us. No one knew where we were. Mom had gone shopping in town, and we hadn't left a note telling her where we were going. Sure, she'd figure out that we went for a bike ride. But the chances of her—or anyone, for that matter—searching for us in an old ghost town were slim.

But if we followed the mine, we risked getting lost. We might walk for days. Without water, we would die of dehydration. I'd read somewhere that humans can live for three to four weeks without food, but only three to four days without water.

"Let's follow the mine shaft," Calvin suggested. He tilted his head back and looked up. "There's no way we can climb out of here. We have to follow the mine and hope we find a way out somewhere."

My brother was right. We had only two choices, and while neither option was a good one, following the mine would at least take us somewhere. Obviously, there was a way out.

We just had to find it.

"Then, let's get going," I said.

We had to move a few of the slats out of our way, but we did so without too much difficulty. Then, after taking a few steps, we were completely in the mine and could no longer see the light streaming down from above, from where we had fallen. The blackness before us seemed endless, and Calvin's tiny flashlight wasn't much comfort.

"I'm scared," Calvin said.

"I am, too," I admitted. "But we'll be all right. This has to lead somewhere. We'll find a way out."

Calvin aimed the flashlight beam on the ground beneath us. The stone was hard and fairly flat, as opposed to the walls around us, which were jagged and rocky.

And I know this is going to sound weird, but the silence seemed to speak to me. It was so very, very quiet. There were no sounds, except for our feet scuffing on the rock beneath us. I don't think I've ever experienced such complete and total silence.

While we walked, we talked. We spoke about going to the beach, hiking in the woods, all of the things that we enjoyed doing. We talked about things that we would do after we got out of the mine. For the most part, we talked about anything to keep our minds off our situation.

Finally, we came to a place in the mine where another tunnel split off to the right. We stopped, wondering which way to go.

Calvin raised the flashlight, sweeping the small beam around.

"I was hoping to find a sign," he said. "You know . . . something with an arrow pointing toward a way out."

I hadn't really thought about that, but it was an interesting point. You would think that the miners would've put up signs so that they didn't get lost.

"Which way should we go?" I asked.

Calvin shined the light down the mine that led to the left, and he swept the beam over to the tunnel that stretched off to the right.

"Like Mom says: six of one, half-dozen of the other. I'm not sure it matters."

"Yes, it does," I said. "One of these tunnels might lead us out in a couple of hundred feet. The other one might take us miles into the ground."

Calvin swept the light back to the left.

"Let's go this way," he said. "It's better than—"

Suddenly, something caught my attention in the mine shaft that stretched off to the right.

Something that shouldn't be there.

I grasped Calvin's arm.

"Look at that!" I said. *"Do you see it!"*

Calvin gasped. "I see it," he said, "but I don't believe it."

Far off in the mine shaft that stretched off to the right was a faint, flickering, orange glow!

10

What we were seeing didn't seem possible. Here we were, underground in a mine shaft, and we were seeing a light. It wasn't sunlight, and it appeared to be moving.

That could mean only one thing: we weren't alone in the mines. There were other humans here, too.

"There's somebody there," Calvin said in disbelief. "I thought all the mines were supposed to be closed up and sealed shut."

"Me, too," I said. "But if there's someone else in the mines, they must know a way out. Come on! Let's go ask him for help!"

We hurried down the tunnel that led off to the right, not able to go very fast, because Calvin's light wasn't very bright, and we had to be careful where we walked. Already, both of us had stumbled on jagged chunks of stone and nearly fallen.

Ahead of us, the light had vanished, but I knew that, whoever it was, they hadn't gone far.

"Hey!" I shouted. "Can anybody hear me?"

I stopped and grabbed Calvin's arm, signaling for him to stop, too.

We stood in the gloom, listening.

"Hello?" I said. "Is there anybody there? Can anyone hear me?"

We listened, but heard nothing.

"They must not be able to hear us," Calvin said. "But whoever it is, they can't be far."

We started walking again, taking long

strides, watching the ground in front of our feet, while, at the same time, glancing up to look into the darkness of the tunnel to see any signs of the mysterious, orange light.

"I wonder who it is?" I said. "It seems strange that there would be somebody else in the mine. I didn't think they were used for anything anymore."

"Maybe there's still some copper left, after all," Calvin said. "Maybe someone is mining it."

We continued walking at a hurried pace. I stumbled once, but I caught myself before I fell.

Finally, we stopped and listened once again.

"Turn your flashlight off," I said.

Calvin did as I asked, and the blackness was unlike anything I'd ever experienced. It seemed strange to have my eyes wide open and not be able to see any sign of light whatsoever.

And there was no sign of the mysterious, orange light.

"It's like they vanished," Calvin said.

"Hello?" I said loudly. My voice echoed

through the tunnel until it finally died out. There was no response.

"Maybe we just imagined it," Calvin said.

"No," I replied. "We both saw it."

"Hey!" Calvin shouted so loudly that I jumped. "Who's down here?!?!"

This time, we *did* hear something, but it didn't sound like a human. It was a strange growl, deep and gruff. I'd never heard anything like it, and the snarl sent a wave of chills through my entire body.

What in the world was that? I wondered. *Who—or what—else was down here in the mine?*

Some sort of animal, I was sure.

But what about the light? We'd seen a strange light flickering, for sure. Animals don't have any use for lights.

The snarl came again, and Calvin turned on his flashlight. A flat, white circle appeared on the stone in front of us.

"I don't like the sound of that," I said. "Maybe we should go the other way. Whatever it is, it doesn't sound human."

A shuffling sound came from deep in the mine, where the snarl had come from.

Then, we saw a faint, orange light. It was far away, and we couldn't see what the source was, but I was starting to get a really bad feeling about it.

"Let's go back," I whispered. *"I'm not sure I want to know what that is."*

"Wait a second," Calvin said. "It's got to be somebody else. And if there's someone else down here, they must know the way out."

"Did you hear that sound?" I asked. "That didn't sound like it came from a human. That sounded like it came from an animal of some sort."

"Maybe it was just a dog," Calvin said.

"No dog I've ever heard makes a sound like that," I said. "And how would a dog get into a mine shaft?"

The orange glow became brighter and brighter. Then, we saw something solid, shiny like metal, but glowing orange, giving off its own light.

"What in the—"

Calvin swallowed his words and stopped speaking.

A bad day was about to get much worse.

"*I can't believe what I'm seeing!*" I hissed.

Calvin remained silent, pointing his small flashlight at the ground in front of us.

I grabbed him by the arm. "*Come on!*" I said. "*Let's go back!*"

We turned and ran, but we couldn't go very fast in the darkness. Calvin's flashlight didn't provide much light, but I was thankful that he brought it anyway. Without it, we wouldn't have attempted to try to find our way through the mine shafts.

Maybe that wasn't such a good idea, either, I thought.

My mind raced, trying to figure out exactly what it was that we had seen. He was definitely human-like in the fact that he had two legs, two arms, and some sort of head, but very little, if any, neck. He was all shiny and orange, glowing like a new penny.

That word—penny—made me think of something else.

Copper.

We were in a copper mine, and the creature—or whatever he was—looked like he could have been made of copper.

But copper isn't alive, I thought. *Copper is a metal. Not only is it used to make pennies, but we learned in school that copper is used as a conductor for electricity and heat, and it's used to make pipes and wiring.*

All of these thoughts whirled through my

brain as we hastily made our way back through the tunnel. If there was one good thing, it was the fact that we seemed to be a bit faster than the glowing monster; when I shot a glance over my shoulder, I could no longer see him. I could still see the mine shaft glowing orange, and I knew the creature was still coming toward us, but we had been able to put some distance between us and him.

"Wait!" Calvin said as he stopped. He shined his light to the side where yet another tunnel appeared. This one was smaller than the one we were in, but it was still big enough for us to enter, if we went in one at a time. Also, it appeared that the tunnel slanted downward, deeper into the earth.

"Let's go in there!" Calvin said.

"But we don't know where it goes!" I protested. "It might just be a dead end!"

"That doesn't matter," Calvin said. "That thing that's after us is pretty big, and I don't think he'll be able to come after us if we go in there."

Calvin had a good point. Maybe if we

crawled into the smaller tunnel, the glowing, orange thing might not even know we were there.

Calvin slipped into the tunnel, and I followed. It angled down steeply, and I used my hands to brace myself against each rock wall, so I wouldn't lose my footing.

Then, I bumped into Calvin.

"This is as far as it goes," he said. "It's a dead end, after all."

I turned around and looked up.

Where the opening of the narrow tunnel was, we could see a faint, orange glow, but it was getting brighter and brighter. The monster was still coming, but if we were lucky, he would pass right by and not even know we were there.

But we weren't going to be so lucky.

12

Calvin and I crouched low at the bottom of the mine shaft, facing the entrance. He switched off his flashlight, and we waited, breathless, as the orange glow became brighter and brighter. All the while, we could hear the creature coming closer. He didn't make the sound of footsteps, but more like a scuffing of boots shuffling along.

And he was making strange grunting sounds and low growls every few seconds.

Then, his massive shape suddenly filled the entrance to our narrow passageway . . . and stopped. Bright orange light spilled into the tunnel where we were hiding, causing the jagged rock walls to appear dark rust in color. It was the first time we'd been able to get a good look at the inside of one of the tunnels.

Keep going, I thought, as if the coppery beast would hear me and continue on his way. *Just keep going and leave us alone.*

Beside me, I felt Calvin cringe. His entire body stiffened.

"What is that thing?" he whispered.

"I don't know," I replied quietly. *"Some sort of creature. He looks like he's made out of copper."*

Which, of course, was impossible.

Was it?

Slowly, the creature turned, and I could see his hideous face. It was round-shaped, except for the top of his head, which was almost triangular. His eyes were nothing more than wide slits, barely open, with thick, hairless eyebrows.

Strangest of all was his mouth. It was rectangular, wide-open, and glowing even brighter than his skin, as if he had a candle in his mouth. He had no lips and no teeth, and the top of his head appeared as though it was melting, with coppery goo dripping over his forehead like candle wax.

And he had no nose. At least not a nose I could see.

How on Earth does he breathe? I wondered. *Does he even breathe at all?* I never knew such a creature existed, and I wondered why I'd never heard of this thing before. It was as if he was a copper-colored Bigfoot. I read a book one time about a couple of kids in Idaho who came across a creature in the woods called an 'ice beast.' The book was pretty freaky, but that's all it was: a book. The story freaked me out, but it was nothing compared to what I was feeling, crouched at the bottom of the narrow tunnel, looking up at the gigantic orange monster peering down at us.

"Do you think he sees us?" Calvin whispered.

"I don't know," I replied quietly. *"But I think you're right. I don't think he can get at us because he's too big."*

As if the horrible beast heard us, he slowly backed up . . . but he wasn't leaving. He was only giving himself enough room to reach out with his arm, which easily fit into the tunnel. He reached down toward us.

"I'm glad his arms aren't any longer," I said.

His hand was large, the size of a baseball glove. It reached down toward us, but never came close. Instead, his hand pressed against the jagged stone and felt around, as if he thought he might be able to grab one of us.

Finally, he withdrew his arm.

"What is that thing?" Calvin whispered, repeating his earlier question. His voice trembled with fear. *"It's like some creature from a comic book."*

That was a good description. Whatever this monster was, I could easily see him doing battle with a superhero in some comic book or cartoon.

But that didn't take away from the fact that we were scared to death. Reading a comic book or watching television is fine, because if you get scared, you can just walk away.

Here, backed into a corner in a narrow mine shaft, we couldn't walk away. There was nowhere for us to go.

Finally, the creature withdrew his arm and peered back into the tunnel where we were hiding.

"*I don't think he can see us,*" Calvin whispered. "*It's like he knows we're here, but he can't see us.*"

I hoped my brother was right. Maybe the creature, whatever he was, would continue on his way. We wouldn't be out of danger, of course. But it would be one less thing to worry about, for the time being.

However, as it would turn out, we had a lot more to worry about than just being lost in the copper mines and being stalked by a glowing, orange beast. In minutes, we were about to find out what the word 'terror' really meant.

13

Seeing the creature draw back and move away, continuing on through the shaft, in the direction we had just come from was like a dream come true. Calvin and I waited in the darkness, staring up the narrow tunnel, watching the orange glow until it vanished.

"You think he's gone?" Calvin asked.

"Where is he going to go?" I replied. "Whatever he is, he probably lives down here in the mines."

"What if there are more?" Calvin asked.

"There might be," I replied. "We're going to have to watch out for them."

Calvin clicked on his small flashlight, and we scrambled up the narrow passageway, stopping at the wider mine shaft. We were cautious, looking both ways to make sure we didn't see the strange, coppery glow that could come only from the hideous creature we'd just seen.

"Let's go that way," Calvin said, sweeping his flashlight to the left.

"I'm not sure that's a good idea," I said. "That's where that creature came from."

"If we go that way," Calvin said, sweeping the flashlight to the right, "we might run into him. There might be only one of them, and I don't want to be following him."

My brother had a good point.

"Okay," I agreed. "Let's go that way."

We scrambled from the narrow passageway into the mine shaft.

"Go slow," I said. "We have to be on the lookout for any more of those things."

We walked at a turtle's pace, being careful not to make any noise with our shoes. Once in a while, a few pieces of gravel would crunch beneath our feet, but it wasn't very loud.

Soon, we came to an intersection in the mine shaft. Not only did it continue in front of us, but the mine continued to the right and to our left. Not only that, but the shaft that intersected with the one we had been walking in had train tracks.

Calvin knelt down and shined his light on the rusty metal.

"This track has to lead out of here," he said.

"The problem is," I said, "which way do we go?"

Calvin shined his light along the wall, aiming it higher and higher.

"Look!" he suddenly shouted, and I could see the glow of his face as he tilted his head back and looked up.

I stared up into the darkness.

"There's nothing to see," I said.

"Exactly!" Calvin replied. "There's a shaft that goes straight up! And look!"

He shined the light higher, and the beam fell upon jagged rock . . . and something else.

A ladder! There was a ladder embedded in the rock! The rungs were made of metal, and they stretched up until they vanished in the darkness.

Calvin reached up and grasped the bottom rung.

"Here," he said, and he handed me his tiny flashlight. "Hang on to this."

I shined the light on his back as he pulled himself up, pressing his feet against the uneven rock wall until he was able to put one of his shoes on the bottom rung.

"I'll climb up a ways and see where this goes," he said.

"You're not going to see anything," I said. "It's too dark."

"Maybe so," Calvin replied. By now, he was fading into the inky darkness. "But this shaft might lead right up to the surface. We can't be far."

Calvin was right. We hadn't fallen very far, and I knew that we must be close to the surface.

"Be careful," I said.

I could no longer see my brother, but I could hear him scrambling up the ladder. After a few moments, I could no longer hear anything.

"Are you all right?" I shouted. My voice echoed all around me, fading away in every mine shaft.

"I'm fine," came Calvin's reply from high above. His voice sounded thin and hollow in the narrow shaft. "But it sure is dark."

I shut off the flashlight to save the battery. There was no telling how long we would be in the mines, and I didn't want to waste the flashlight's energy. We might need it longer than we thought.

Once again, I was immersed in total darkness. It was a strange, lonely feeling to be isolated, underground, and alone.

Then again, I really wasn't alone. My brother was above me on the ladder . . . but from behind me, I heard the crunching of stone and gravel.

I turned to see a faint, coppery glow far off in the mine shaft.

And it was growing brighter by the second.

14

"Calvin!" I shouted.

No answer.

I snapped my head around. The orange glow was getting brighter, and I knew it was only a matter of time before the horrible creature came into view.

So, I did the only thing I could do: I climbed.

Reaching up into the darkness, I found the ladder. Grasping the bottom rung with both hands,

I began pulling myself up, using my feet against the wall of the shaft until I was able to put my right shoe on the bottom rung. I continued pulling myself up, climbing in the darkness. It was scary, not being able to see anything. But I couldn't just stand there in the mine shaft and be a sitting duck for that copper creature. All I could do was climb up and hope that thing couldn't follow me.

"*Calvin!*" I shouted again.

This time, he heard me.

"*What?*" my brother shouted down to me.

"*I'm coming up!*" I shouted. "*That thing is coming!*"

I had a moment of panic when my left foot slipped off the rung, but I had a firm grip with my hands, and I didn't fall.

Then, I heard Calvin shout something, and it sounded like a dream.

"There's daylight above! I can see daylight!"

Finally! I thought, with an enormous wave of relief. *Now, we can get out of here. We can go home. We can get away from that horrible orange creature.*

I found renewed strength in Calvin's words, and I began climbing as fast as I dared in the total blackness.

"What do you see?" I shouted. I was anxious to know more. It seemed like hours since I had been in the daylight, the sunshine warming my skin.

"I can see light up above," Calvin replied. "It's definitely a way out of here, but it looks like it's sealed off with boards."

That's no big deal, I thought. *We can always break the wood. It's probably old and rotting, anyway.*

I continued to climb carefully until I could see the faint light above. But it was more than daylight; it was hope. Before, we had faced the very real possibility of being stuck in the mines without anyone finding us. Now, we were only minutes from safety, minutes from leaving the mines and that horrible, glowing copper creature behind.

The higher I climbed, the brighter the light became, and I could finally make out Calvin's silhouette as he made his way to the mouth of the shaft. By now, I could clearly see daylight streaming through the wood slats. My brother began pounding on the old beams, and I continued to climb.

"It's not boarded up with wood!" Calvin cried out, and I could hear the despair in his voice.

"What is it?" I shouted. He was only about twenty feet above me, and I was trying not to think about how far I'd climbed, how high I was in the mine shaft. If I lost my grip and fell, it would be all over.

"Metal!" Calvin said, and I heard him slapping the steel with his hands. "They put metal bars across the entrance. We'll never be able to break them, and they won't bend!"

I pulled myself up until I was right below my brother, and I couldn't go any farther because the only thing to hold on to was the ladder. I couldn't help him try to get out even if I wanted to.

"We're not getting out this way," Calvin said. "There's no way we can bend or break this metal."

My heart fell. When I'd first heard Calvin say that he'd spotted light coming from above, my hopes had soared like a plane. Now, that hopeful plane had fallen from the sky and come crashing back to Earth.

But what made matters worse?

Far below us, in the darkness of the mine shaft, we saw an orange glow slowly getting brighter and brighter.

The creature was climbing up the ladder . . . and there was nowhere for us to go.

15

"That thing is coming!" I shouted. *"He's climbing up after us!"*

"Go back down!" Calvin shouted.

"Are you nuts?!?!" I shouted back.

"Go down just a few feet," Calvin said. "There's a mine shaft that goes off to the side. It's right below you."

I snapped my head around and looked down. Sure enough, in the dim sunlight streaming through the bars, I could see a gaping black hole, a wide tunnel that bored horizontally into the earth. Although I could now see it in the dim light, I had missed it on my way up, because I'd been so frantic.

I clambered down a couple of rungs and placed one foot in the tunnel, mindful that one little slip would mean the end for me.

There were several pieces of metal protruding from the side of the shaft, and I grasped one of them with my left hand and pulled, letting go of the ladder and slipping into the tunnel. Calvin quickly followed, and we peered down into the deep, cavernous shaft we'd just left.

Far below us, we could see the coppery shape of the creature, glowing like the sun, climbing up. He seemed slow and a bit cumbersome, but he was still coming for us, and we needed to get moving.

"Do you still have my flashlight?" Calvin asked.

I pulled the light from my pocket and gave

it to him. He clicked it on and shined it into the shaft we'd just entered.

Steel railroad tracks stretched into the empty, beckoning darkness. There were a few pieces of rusting metal pipes and rotting wooden beams scattered about on the rocky ground. The walls around and above were jagged and rough, the work of man and machine as they chewed through the earth in search of copper.

"We're only a few feet underground," Calvin said. "This might lead to a way out."

"I'm sure it does," I said. "But it might go on for miles and miles."

"We don't have a choice," Calvin said. He started walking, aiming the beam on the rock floor at our feet. I followed as we walked between the steel rails.

All the while, I was well aware that the glowing creature was climbing up the shaft, and the farther we got away from him, the better. I had tons of questions: *What was he? Where did he come from? Does anyone else know about him?*

But none of those questions mattered now. Now, the only question that mattered was: *can we get away from him?*

The tunnel began a wide turn to the left, and we continued on. With only the faint glow of the tiny flashlight, it was difficult to see anything more than the ground, our shoes, and the two metal tracks as they wound through the shaft like old steel snakes.

"I hope that battery lasts," I said.

"It's an LED light," Calvin replied. "Mom said the battery is supposed to last a long time."

I glanced over my shoulder and looked behind me, thankful to see only inky blackness.

But when I turned back around, I almost walked into a solid wall.

"Whoa," Calvin said. He, too, was surprised at what appeared in front of us. We could walk no farther, and we stopped.

It was a large, wood door with a metal knob the size of a baseball.

"What's a door like this doing in a mine

shaft?" I asked.

"I don't know much about mining," Calvin said as he swept the flashlight beam around the door. Then, he shined it down.

"And look," he said. "The tracks stop right at the door."

I grasped the knob, and it turned easily in my hand.

I pushed the door. Hinges squeaked and squealed as it opened.

Light suddenly spilled in . . . but it wasn't daylight. I kept pushing the door until it was fully open, staring in utter disbelief at what I was seeing.

16

The light we were seeing didn't come from the sun, and the door certainly didn't lead to a way out of the mine shaft.

Instead, we were looking into a large room filled with old, wooden crates. A single light dangled from above, glowing yellow beneath its cone-shaped lamp. On the other side of the room, a wheelbarrow-sized flatbed cart with metal wheels sat on two train tracks that vanished into a smaller, narrow shaft. I'd seen carts like this before on television, usually in old movies. These carts were like human-powered rail cars, with a flatbed and a T-shaped handle in the middle for one or two people—one on either side—to pump up and down. This action made the cart move along the train tracks.

"*What is this place?*" I whispered. "*I thought these mines were abandoned years and years ago.*"

Calvin shook his head. "Somebody must be down here," he said. "That light would have burned out long ago. And besides: the bulb looks like it's brand new."

"But who's down here?" I wondered aloud. "And what are they doing?"

"Your guess is as good as mine," Calvin said.

Behind us, I heard a noise. We both turned to see the now familiar orange glow that could mean only one thing: the copper creature was getting closer.

"Let's get inside and close the door," I said. "Maybe it locks, and we can keep him out."

We hurried through the doorway, and Calvin closed the door. Sure enough, there was a big deadbolt, and I slid it into the locked position.

"I hope that keeps him out," I said. "But just in case, let's get away from the door."

We walked through the cavern to the other side, stopping by the cart on the railroad tracks.

"If that thing breaks down the door," Calvin said, pointing at the cart, "that's our only way out."

I looked into the shaft. The two steel rails disappeared into darkness.

Now that we were in the room, we took a better look at our surroundings.

It wasn't really a room as much as it was a cave. It had been carved out like a room, but it was shaped like a box. The walls and ceiling were flat, but there were still parts that were uneven due to the jagged rock. The floor, although relatively flat, was also uneven.

"Somebody spent a lot of time blasting and chipping away rock to make this room," Calvin said as he turned off his flashlight and tucked it into the pocket of his jeans.

To the right of us, there were two stacks of large, wooden crates. They didn't appear to be all that old, in comparison to just about everything else we saw in the mines.

"I wonder what's in them," I said.

Calvin shook his head. "No idea," he replied.

On the other side of the cavernous room came a soft pound on the door, causing us both to flinch.

"It's that thing!" Calvin hissed. *"He's trying to get in here!"*

"The door is bolted," I said. "Let's hope that it—"

There was a sudden, loud explosion of splintering wood as the door was ripped from its hinges. There was still another loud sound as the door slammed to the rock surface.

And standing in the doorway was the hideous copper creature.

17

There's nothing like the feeling of being trapped, of having nowhere to go, nowhere to run. Our only option was to climb onto the cart on the track and flee through the shaft. I didn't think the tunnel was big enough for the giant creature, but I didn't want to take any chances. We would probably be able to move a lot faster on the cart, because if we had to run or walk, there was always a chance of us tripping and falling. If we stayed on the cart on the tracks, we wouldn't have to worry about tripping.

But there was no way of knowing where the mine shaft led, either, and the flatbed cart looked old. It might not even work.

"Jump on!" I shouted, and we both leapt onto the cart.

"How does this thing work?" Calvin said.

"Grab the handle and pump up and down!" I said frantically. "That's how it moves!"

On the other side of the cavern, the copper creature stood in the doorway, glowing in the single light bulb that dangled from the ceiling.

Then, he took a step toward us.

And another.

I pushed the handle down, and Calvin pulled his side up. Slowly, the cart began to move.

"Faster!" I urged. *"Push down and then pull up! We've got to get this thing moving faster!"*

We entered the dark mine shaft as the cart picked up more and more speed. Behind me, the light from the cavern began to fade as we traveled deeper and deeper into the earth. Then, the entrance to the shaft was covered by the copper creature. Thankfully, I had been right: he was too big to follow us.

The steel wheels screeched and squeaked on the iron tracks. When all light behind us faded, a new light appeared: Calvin's flashlight. A softball-sized disc illuminated the jagged stone walls as we made our way farther into the mine shaft.

"Okay," I said. "Let's slow down. I don't think that thing can follow us in here, and we need to be able to see where we're going. I think I can keep this cart going by myself. You turn around and shine the light on the tracks ahead of us."

Calvin let go of the handle, and I continued to pump up and down. Without my brother's help, it was a little more difficult, but I managed to keep us moving along at a pace a little faster than a walk.

"We'll be able to cover a lot more ground this way," I said. "It's faster than walking, and I'll bet it leads to a way out."

"I just don't want to run into any more of

those things," Calvin said as he held the light in front of him. "Where do you think he came from?"

"A science fiction movie," I said.

From where I was, I could see only Calvin's black silhouette and the faint, white glow of the flashlight in front of him.

But I did notice one very curious thing: it was getting easier and easier to pump the handle and keep us moving. Soon, it was almost no effort at all.

When I finally realized what was happening, I was surprised . . . and a little scared.

"Are we going faster?" Calvin said.

"Yes," I said. "But I'm hardly pumping the handle."

The reason, of course, was that the tracks were slowly sloping steeper and steeper downward, propelling us faster and faster.

"Shine the light back here," I said. "There has to be a brake."

Calvin turned and shined the light directly in my face, blinding me momentarily. I raised my hand and shaded my eyes.

"Knock it off," I snapped.

"Sorry," Calvin replied.

He lowered the light and swept the beam across the flatbed. There was a handle that protruded up at an angle, and I was sure it was the brake. Which was a good thing, because we were rapidly picking up speed.

I grasped the handle and pulled, and the cart began to slow.

But not for long. There was a sudden snapping sound, a sharp, metal-on-metal squeal, and the handle came off in my hand.

The brake—our only way of stopping the cart—was broken.

18

By now, the cart was moving dangerously fast . . . too fast to even jump off without getting seriously hurt. My brother's tiny light made the jagged rock walls appear only as a blur as we raced through the shaft.

"*Stop this thing!*" Calvin shouted.

"*I can't!*" I shouted back.

We were being pulled along, faster and faster, by the sheer force of gravity, farther and farther, deeper and deeper.

"I have a really, really bad feeling about this!" I shouted.

"You and me both!" Calvin shouted back.

Wind whistled past my ears, and my hair was tossed wildly about. Calvin's flashlight gave us only a glimpse of the walls of the mine shaft as we continued on our deadly roller coaster ride of terror.

"Can you see anything ahead of us?" I shouted.

"The flashlight isn't strong enough!" Calvin shouted back. *"Everything is a blur!"*

The feeling of complete helplessness was overwhelming. If we jumped off the cart, we would be seriously hurt, or worse. Still, if we remained on it, we were at the mercy of wherever the tracks led.

Moments later, I realized we were slowing. Gradually, my fears began to subside.

"I think we're slowing down," Calvin said.

"The tracks are probably leveling out," I said. "Can you see anything at all with that flashlight?"

"Just the tracks in front of us," Calvin said.

Soon, the cart had come to a complete stop. We were on level ground in the mine shaft once again.

I stepped off the cart and stood. There was just enough room for me to stand up without having to bend over.

"I have to get off this thing, at least for a minute," I said. "That was the scariest roller coaster ride I've ever been on."

"Yeah," Calvin agreed. "But thankfully, there were no turns or loops."

"If there had been turns or loops," I said, "we would have been tossed off that thing. We would have been hurt."

Calvin scrambled off the cart and walked around it. He stopped next to me and shined the tiny flashlight beam around the mine shaft.

"What do you want to do?" he asked.

I thought for a moment. I really wasn't sure what to do. It might be too dangerous to continue on with the cart. But, then again, the cart allowed us to travel faster than we would if we were walking.

But then Calvin shined his light on something that changed everything . . . .

19

When Calvin swept his flashlight beam on the ground, we saw something shiny, reflecting the light.

"Hey," Calvin said. "What's that?"

We both knelt down, stunned to find an ordinary set of keys on the chipped, rocky ground.

I picked them up, and they jangled in my hand. There were seven keys—three were silver and four were a dull gold color. Strangest of all, the silver keys were shiny and appeared to be brand new.

Calvin kept the flashlight beam trained on the keys in my hand.

"How did a set of new keys get in the mine?" I asked.

"It looks like someone could have dropped them recently," Calvin said.

I continued staring at the wad of keys in my hand.

Keys mean locks, I thought. *And locks mean doors.*

It was just another mystery piled onto all of the others. The biggest mystery, of course, was the strange copper creature itself. What was he, really? Where did he come from? What did he want from us, if anything? There were no answers. Not yet, anyway.

But the discovery of the keys was really puzzling, as it led me to believe that someone else had been in the mines, and probably not long ago. And considering the size of the copper creature's large, bulky hands, I thought it unlikely that the keys would belong to him.

A noise in the mine shaft turned our attention away from the wad of keys in my hand. Calvin trained the beam of light down the tunnel, but it was too faint to do anything more than illuminate the area a few feet around us.

"Did you hear that?" Calvin whispered.

"Shhh," I whispered back. *"Listen. And turn your light off."*

When Calvin turned off his flashlight, we were once again immersed in an uncomfortable, inky blackness . . . but not for long. Soon, we could see the now familiar faint, orange glow in the mine shaft.

The copper creature was coming.

Again.

"I didn't think this shaft was big enough for that thing to follow us," Calvin said.

"That doesn't matter now," I replied. "What matters is where we're going to go."

"Should we get on the cart?" Calvin asked.

I thought about this. After our harrowing ride only minutes before, I wasn't sure if riding on the cart was the best idea. True, we would go faster riding the rails than our feet would carry us, but we had no idea where the tracks went. I would hate to go plummeting down the shaft, uncontrolled and unable to stop. That might be worse than falling into the clutches of that horrible orange creature.

"Let's leave the cart here," I said. "We won't be able to go as fast on foot, but I think we'll be safer."

Calvin turned on his flashlight, and we carefully made our way around to the other side of the cart and began following the tracks deeper and deeper into the mine shaft.

"If Mom knew what we were doing right now," Calvin said as we walked, "she would ground us for a month."

"Maybe," I replied. "But it's hardly our fault. We had no idea that the side of the mine would collapse, and we'd fall into it."

Every few moments, I looked over my

shoulder, gazing behind us into the darkness. I no longer saw the faint, orange glow, and I was glad that we were putting some distance between us and the creature.

Suddenly, the mine shaft ended at a solid wall made of wood. The tracks at our feet stopped a few feet before it.

Calvin got closer and shined his light all around.

"Hey!" he said. "This is a door! Look! There's a handle, right there!"

He trained his beam at a brass knob on the door. It was shiny and new and reflected the flashlight beam. Calvin grasped the knob and tried to turn it.

"It's locked," he said.

I was still holding the set of keys in my hand, and I held them out.

Behind us, I heard a noise. Calvin and I turned.

Far off in the shaft, we saw the orange glow again.

"Try one of those keys!" Calvin hissed. *"Hurry!"*

I approached the door and tried a key in the lock, but it wouldn't turn. Then, I tried another one. And another one.

"Hurry up!" Calvin said. "That thing is getting closer!"

Finally, one of the keys turned. There was a metallic clicking sound as the lock disengaged. I turned the knob and opened the door . . . but Calvin and I were totally unprepared for what was on the other side.

20

The door opened into an enormous cavern, but it was the gigantic contraption before us that took my breath away.

It was a tube-like vehicle of some sort, as big as a semi truck and just as tall. There were no doors or windows that we could see and no wheels. On one end, to our right, the contraption was rounded. At the other end, however, a long, pointed cone extended out like a long screw with a sharp point, which was buried part way into the rock wall, as if it had been in the process of boring into it, but was now stopped. It was the strangest thing I think I've ever seen in my life . . . but I was getting used to seeing strange things.

"Wow, Mikayla," Calvin said. "What is this thing?"

"I don't know," I said, shaking my head. "It almost looks like some sort of spacecraft."

"Not a spacecraft," Calvin said. "It looks more like a submarine with an ice cream cone on one end."

Calvin was right. It really *did* resemble a submarine of some sort.

But what's it doing here, in the copper mine shafts beneath Calumet? I wondered. What it was doing in the mines was anybody's guess. I certainly didn't have an answer.

We didn't see any movement anywhere, so I stuffed the wad of keys into my front pocket and slowly began to make my way around the large vessel. Calvin followed close behind.

"You're right, Calvin," I said. "It really does look like some sort of submarine."

"But that doesn't make sense," Calvin said, scratching his head. "Submarines belong in the ocean."

"Maybe it's some sort of old mining device," I said. "You know, something that's used to penetrate deep into the earth, like a giant drill. That nose cone looks like it's made for drilling into rock."

When we reached what I thought was the rear of the contraption, we stopped and looked down the gaping tunnel, which was perfectly round, and the exact same height and width of the vessel.

Calvin spoke. "I think you're right, Mikayla," he said. "I think it's a machine that goes through the ground like a giant worm."

"It must be something used by miners," I said.

Calvin shook his head. "I don't know much about copper mining," he said. "Only what we've learned in school. But I don't think the miners used anything like this. I've seen lots of old pictures of working copper mines before, but I've never seen one of these before."

On the other side of the strange machine was an open door and a series of metal stairs cascading down to the ground; the same kind of steps you'd find on some airplanes. Cautiously, I made my way slowly up the steps and peered inside the vessel. Calvin followed at my heels.

"Wow," he breathed over my shoulder.

This is incredible, I thought. *I've never seen anything like this before in my life.*

What we were looking at appeared to be the inside of a spacecraft of some sort. Of course, that's probably not what it was. I've never been in a spacecraft, but I've seen enough television shows to know that the cockpits of rockets and spaceships contain complicated gadgetry . . . like what we were seeing right now.

Near the front, to our right, were two leather seats affixed to thick metal posts bolted to the floor. In front of the seats was a panel containing all sorts of levers and buttons. In the middle, between the two seats, was what appeared to be a large joystick, and I assumed that it was used to control the vessel.

"This is incredible," Calvin said quietly.

I shook my head. "Things just gets stranger and stranger," I said.

We were so engrossed in what we were seeing, so focused on the incredible sight before us, that we failed to hear the noise behind us, in the cavern . . . until it was too late.

21

I heard a noise, and out of the corner of my eye, I saw something move. Turning, I was horrified to see not one, but two horrible orange creatures only a few feet away from the mysterious craft. They stood their ground, motionless. Both were looking at us.

When Calvin turned and saw them, he yelped and leapt back away from the open door.

"We're trapped inside this thing!" he shouted.

"There's nowhere to go!"

Frantically, I began searching for a way to close the door of the vessel. If the creatures prevented us from leaving the strange craft, maybe we could at least keep the creatures from getting inside.

Near the open doorway was a panel with several buttons. I pressed a couple of them, but nothing happened.

"What are you doing?!?!" Calvin shrieked.

"I'm trying to find a way to close this door!" I shouted. *"There's got to be some way to close it!"*

I kept randomly pressing buttons, hoping something would happen. Meanwhile, the horrific copper creatures slowly moved toward us.

Suddenly, there was a metallic humming sound. The steps quickly folded up and a metal panel began sliding over the opening, closing like an elevator door. The doorway began to get smaller. One of the buttons I had pressed worked.

However, the strange copper creatures had already reached the craft. One of them had his arm through the doorway, and he was trying to push the panel back, trying to stop it from closing.

Thankfully, he wasn't strong enough. I was surprised when the door continued to close and the creature was forced to withdraw his hand. Seconds later, the door clicked completely shut with a solid, satisfying *thunk*.

Outside the vessel, the creatures began pounding on the door and the sides of the craft.

"Do you think they can get in?" Calvin asked.

"I have no idea," I replied, shaking my head. "I hope not."

Soon, the pounding on the sides of the craft ceased. Because there were no windows, we couldn't see what was going on. All we could do was wait as the seconds ticked past, breathless, listening for anything. We had no idea whether the copper creatures were still around or not.

Finally, after not hearing any more noises for a few minutes, Calvin walked to the front of the craft, to the cockpit, and sat down in one of the chairs. I followed.

"Strange," I said.

"What's strange?" Calvin asked. "I mean, besides *everything?*"

I pointed at the switches and dials and levers on the large, wide panel before us.

"Look at all this stuff," I said. "All of the knobs and levers and buttons are small."

Calvin shrugged. "So?" he said.

"Well," I continued, "think about it: those creatures' hands are big and bulky. They would have a hard time flipping switches and pressing buttons, because their fingers are so fat."

"So what does that mean?" Calvin asked.

"It means that this craft was made by someone else," I answered. "Probably a human being."

"This is so whacked-out," Calvin said. "If you had told me that my day was going to turn out like this, I would've said you were crazy."

"Same here," I said.

"Hey," Calvin said as he turned toward me. "Suppose that—"

There was a sudden loud, churning sound, and the entire craft shook.

"What's going on?" I said, grasping the seat.

Calvin looked down. "I think my knee bumped something on the front panel," he said.

Somewhere within the vessel, a powerful engine roared like a lion. It revved once, twice, three times, and then settled into a lower idle.

A new sound suddenly erupted in front of us. It sounded like another motor, but it was deeper and rougher and sounded like metal grinding against metal. The entire vessel shook even more.

"Let's get out of this thing!" Calvin shouted above the roaring noise.

"We can't!" I shouted back. *"Those things might still be out there!"*

A sudden movement rocked the vessel, and there was no mistake: we had started moving forward. In my mind, I could see the strange, pointed tip of the craft. I envisioned it spinning around and around, and that's when I realized what was about to happen.

I knew it! I thought. *We're inside of a drill! That's what this machine is for! It's not only a vessel of some sort, it's a drill, designed to bore through the earth!*

But I also realized something else.

We knew nothing about the machine. We had no idea how to stop it, no idea how to control it. The only thing we could do was sit in our seats and hang on.

22

I think what drove me crazy was the fact that I couldn't see where we were going. I was certain that we were pressing forward. But not knowing where we were headed, not being able to see anything besides the interior of the craft was maddening . . . and not being able to control it was even worse.

There was a heavy banging noise in front of us, and the craft lurched to a brief halt. The sound coming from in front of us, the twisting and turning of the cone, became louder, more violent.

Then, we were moving again, pressing forward. All the while, the craft rocked and shook, tossing us about in our seats.

"We're boring through the rock!" I said to Calvin. "That cone in front of us is like a drill. It's spinning around, chewing a hole through the ground!"

Calvin frantically looked around. "There's got to be a way to stop this thing!" he said.

I joined the search. We looked for anything that might shut off the motor. I looked for a switch, for a button that read STOP—anything. I was sure that what we were looking for was right in front of us, but we couldn't see it. After all: we had no idea what to look for.

Meanwhile, the vessel continued to churn and tremble as we bored deeper and deeper into the ground. It was impossible to tell how fast we were moving, but the grinding sound in front of us was louder than ever. I was certain that it took an immense amount of power for the cone to spin, to chew up the rock and drill a hole big enough for the vessel to fit through.

Whoever invented this is a genius, I thought. *Or a madman. Maybe both.*

Calvin grabbed the metal handle that was positioned between the two seats. He moved it from side to side, then forward and back, like a giant joystick. As he did, I could feel the vessel turning to the left and to the right, then angling down and back up again.

"This is how you steer this thing!" Calvin said, excitedly. He shifted the handle to the right, and we could feel the vessel slowly turn in that direction.

Then, I discovered something else. On the control panel in front of me was a small computer screen. The screen itself was dark, but bright green lines crisscrossed each other at different angles. Near the center of the screen was a blinking red dot. It was moving slowly, trailing a green line.

I pointed. "Look!" I said. "I think that's us,

right there! The red dot! We're looking at a radar map of where we are in the ground!"

"That means we can get out of here!" Calvin said. "All we have to do is go up until we break the surface of the earth!"

And with that, Calvin pulled the lever back. We could feel the nose of the vessel begin to rise, and soon, we were headed almost straight up, our backs pressed against the seats. I found a seat belt and latched it around my waist, so I wouldn't fall out of the chair. Calvin, too, found a seat belt and strapped himself in.

"We're as good as home, now!" Calvin said.

It still felt very strange not being able to see where we were going, but I kept watching the blinking red dot on the small computer screen as it continued to move upward. Occasionally, it crisscrossed over other green lines, and I wondered if they represented mine shafts.

Finally, the spinning cone in front of the vessel changed its pitch. It was no longer grinding and chomping, but seemed to be spinning freely.

The craft came to a halt.

"I wish I knew how to shut this thing off," I said.

"Now what do we do?" Calvin said.

We were still pointed almost straight up with our backs pressed against the chairs, which meant that if we released our seat belts, we wouldn't be able to stand up. We'd fall to the back of the craft, which would be a twenty-foot drop. We'd break our legs.

So, we had a problem. The door was behind us, but there was no way to reach it. Gravity would cause us to fall.

We were stuck.

"We have to find a way to reach the door without falling," I said. "While we're stuck in this position, we can't get out of our chairs."

"Do you think we're back on the surface?" Calvin asked.

"We have to be," I replied. "I don't think we're moving because the cone in front is stuck up in the air. That's how this thing moves through the earth. As the cone turns, it's like a drill, pulling the rest of the vessel through the earth."

Then, to our great surprise, the door opened on its own . . . and Calvin and I were shocked to see what was on the other side.

23

As the door slid open, Calvin and I turned in our seats. It was awkward, because we had to turn and look down while we were still strapped in by our seat belts.

I expected to see the horrifying copper creatures, but was totally amazed—and relieved —when the face of a normal man appeared! He was wearing a dark blue, oil-stained jumpsuit. His hair was black and speckled with gray, as was his tightly-trimmed mustache and beard. Thick glasses made his eyes appear larger than normal.

"Children?" he said in puzzled disbelief as he looked up at us. He raised his hands as if he was terribly agitated and confused. His eyes were wide and, magnified by his thick glasses, looked as though they were going to fall out of his head.

Then, he pointed to the panel in front of us.

"There's a red switch next to the screen," he said. "Flip it down."

I reached out and did what he asked. Immediately, the roaring engine sputtered and died.

Then, the man placed his hands on his hips and spoke again.

"What do you think you're doing?" he asked.

I couldn't tell if he was mad or if he was truly curious as to why and how we were in the machine.

"All we're trying to do is get out of these mines and go home," I said. We accidentally fell into a mine shaft, and we weren't able to climb out. We've been wandering through mine shafts all morning, trying to keep away from some creepy, orange creatures that are following us."

The man's brow furrowed, and thin wrinkles appeared.

"They didn't touch you, did they?" he asked, his voice ringing with alarm. His eyes widened even more, and they looked like ping pong balls with pupils the size of pennies. "You didn't come into contact with them, did you?"

Calvin and I shook our heads.

"No," Calvin answered. "But they sure freaked us out."

"How many have you seen?" the man asked.

"Two," I replied. "One kept coming after us, and then there were two."

"There are more than two, I'm afraid," the man said.

"Are they dangerous?" I asked.

The man nodded. "More than you could possibly imagine," he replied. "You two are very lucky. No one should be down here. That's one of the reasons the mines were all closed years ago."

"Then, why are you here?" I asked.

"That's a long story," he said, "and I'll tell you all about it on our way out. But first, let's get you out of those seats and onto solid ground. Do you see the large green button on the panel in front of you?"

Calvin and I turned.

"This one?" I said, pointing to a dark green, bubble-shaped button about the size of a quarter.

"Yes," the man replied. "That's the one. Go ahead and press it."

I pressed the button with my index finger, and the machine roared to life once again. And once again, we began moving, but now the vessel was slowly going backward.

"I'll tell you when to press the button again," the man shouted over the roaring engine. "You can't go backward too far, or the doorway will sink back into the earth, and you won't be able to get out."

I turned and looked back at the man standing outside of the vessel and watched as the doorway slowly began to approach the ground.

"Okay," the man said. "Press the button again."

Once again, I did as he instructed. The vessel lurched to a halt, and the motor ceased.

Now the man was able to reach inside, but we were still strapped in our seats with the vessel pointed upward, and I wasn't sure how we were going to get down and out.

I needn't have worried. The man reached into the contraption and pressed a couple of buttons on a panel near the door. Instantly, the chairs we were seated in began to slide backward, as if they were on a track. When we were level with the ground, he pressed a few more buttons and both seats came to a halt.

This made getting out much easier for us, and I quickly unsnapped the safety belt that was hooked over my waist and easily scrambled out the door. Calvin did the same; however, he had to climb from his seat to the seat I had been sitting in, so he wouldn't fall back into the vessel. Still, he was able to make his way out, and soon, we were standing on the hard, rocky ground, staring up at the wide-eyed man in the dark blue jumpsuit.

We were in a large cavern, and there were several lights strung up by large electrical wires that crisscrossed above.

"You two don't know how lucky you are," he said. "In fact, both of you are lucky to be alive."

"But what *are* those things?" Calvin asked. "Why are they so dangerous?"

"Follow me," the man said. "I'll lead you out of the mine shaft and explain along the way."

Those were the greatest sounding words I think I have ever heard! Finally! We were leaving the mine shafts. We were going home!

"But are we safe now?" I asked.

The man nodded. "Yes," he replied. "You're safe, now."

Looking back, now that I think about it, the man didn't lie to us. He really thought we were safe. He really thought that he was going to lead us safely out of the mine shafts, and we could go home.

Simple as that.

No, he hadn't lied to us about being safe. It's just that he was wrong. We weren't safe at all—not by a long shot.

His name was Mr. Jarmo, and he told us that he had been working in the mines all of his life. He was nearly seventy years old, and he was close to finishing his mission: stopping the copper creatures from entering into the mine shafts from a world deep inside the earth, a world that no one knew about.

"You mean there's some sort of place deep in the ground where those things live?" I asked.

"Yes," Mr. Jarmo said. "Not much is known about them."

We walked through a mine shaft that was lit by small electric lights mounted in the ceiling every ten feet or so. It was a relief not to have to walk in darkness and rely on Calvin's tiny flashlight.

"Oh," I said, digging into my right front pocket. I pulled out a wad of keys and held them up. "Are these yours?"

"You found them!" Mr. Jarmo exclaimed. "My keys! That's what I need to lock the doors that I've built. Once I do that, the copper creatures will no longer be able to enter into the mine shafts. I lost those keys a couple of weeks ago, and I haven't been able to find them."

"But where did those things come from?" Calvin asked.

"Years ago," Mr. Jarmo continued, "when the mines were still open and copper was still being mined, we discovered the creatures. They lived deep in the earth—until we disrupted their home."

"How did you do that?" Calvin asked.

"It was an exploratory drilling attempt to go deeper into the earth than we'd ever attempted, in an effort to find more copper. We had no way of knowing that the creatures existed until we began seeing them climbing up through the mine shafts."

This is totally crazy, I thought. *I've lived here my entire life, and I've never heard anything about copper creatures that live in the ground.*

Still, I knew Mr. Jarmo wasn't making up the story, as Calvin and I both saw the copper creatures with our own eyes. We knew they were real, despite how strange and unbelievable Mr. Jarmo's story might sound.

He told us that no one really knew all that much about the copper creatures, except for one thing: their skin was a combination of copper and some sort of powerful, radioactive acid. Which meant, of course, that if they came into contact with humans, the results would be deadly. That's why the mines were sealed off many years ago: to keep people from entering the shafts and becoming victims.

"How many creatures are there?" Calvin asked.

Mr. Jarmo shook his head. "No one knows," he replied. "There may be a few dozen; there may be a few thousand. However, my best guess is there are at least a few hundred. I've spent my life in these mines, building doors, sealing them up. Still, some of the creatures find their way through."

"But what about that contraption?" I asked.

"You mean the ET-7?" Mr. Jarmo said.

"Whatever that thing is that we rode around in," I continued. "What's that for?"

"I call it the ET-7," Mr. Jarmo explained, with a hint of pride in his voice. "ET stands for Earth Tunneler."

"What about the 7?" Calvin asked.

"That's how long it took me to complete it," Mr. Jarmo explained. "Seven long years building the thing, of trials and errors. Finally, I succeeded. It's still not perfect, but I won't be able to use it as I originally intended."

"What do you mean?" I asked.

"Years ago, after the mines were closed," Mr. Jarmo said, "I dreamed of tunneling into the earth to find out more about the mysterious copper creatures. I wanted to find out exactly what they were and where they came from.

"But I realized very soon that they were too dangerous and that my tunneling into the earth only created more avenues for them to emerge from the depths where they could get into the mine shafts. I will tell you this: from my experience with them, the last thing we need are these copper creatures roaming the mine shafts beneath Calumet. As far as I know, none have ever left the shafts, but if they ever did . . . ."

His voice trailed off, and I realized the seriousness of the situation. Too little was known about the creatures and their habits. If they did leave the mine shafts and emerge on the surface, they could really cause trouble for the people of Calumet and other areas of Michigan's Upper Peninsula.

"Is that why the mines were shut down?"

Calvin asked.

"Exactly," Mr. Jarmo replied, nodding. "I was a foreman at the time, and there were only a few of us who knew about the copper creatures. We knew that if the other miners found out about them, it would spell disaster for Calumet. The town would shut down, and everyone would leave. No one would want to remain in a city knowing that there were dangerous, acid-covered beasts from the inner world threatening to climb to the surface.

"On top of that, we knew that once word got out about the copper creatures, news would spread. People would come from all over to find out more about them. They would descend upon the town and go deep into the mines, digging deeper and deeper. That would be a catastrophe, because we know so little about the copper creatures and how they came to be.

"So, those of us who knew about the creatures swore ourselves to secrecy. We made up a story that the copper had been mined out, and any further efforts wouldn't be worth the time or energy. The mines were closed and the entrances sealed shut. Those of us who knew about the copper creatures didn't say anything to anyone, but we quietly and secretly returned to the mines to descend deep and try to find out how the copper creatures were making their escape from their own inner world. We knew that there was a tunnel or a shaft that connected their world with ours."

"So there are others helping you?" I asked.

Mr. Jarmo shook his head. "For a while, yes," he replied. "But they have all passed on. I am the only one left."

"And you live in the mines?" Calvin asked.

"No," Mr. Jarmo said, shaking his head. "I've created a home in an abandoned building that was once used to house workers. From the outside, it looks like it's falling apart, but from the inside, it's actually quite comfortable, and there is a door inside that gives me direct access to the mines. No one knows I'm there. I do have friends, of course, but no one knows where I live. And I've—"

Suddenly, Mr. Jarmo stopped and seized

each of us by the arm. We stopped and stared ahead. No one said a word, and the silence was heavy and thick.

Then, up ahead, we saw something.

An orange glow.

Which could mean only one thing: a copper creature was blocking our way out!

"Quickly!" Mr. Jarmo said. *"We've got to go back! We've got to get back to the ET-7!"*

"But that's a long way back there!" I said. "Isn't there any place to hide?"

"Not in this shaft!" Mr. Jarmo replied. "We'll have to make it back to the ET-7!"

We started running down the shaft, and our footsteps echoed off the rock walls.

I was scared, and I was frustrated. I had thought that we were finally on our way home. Turns out, the real adventure—the real nightmare—hadn't even begun.

But it was about to.

25

It took us a few minutes to return to the ET-7—
which wasn't all that long—but it seemed like
forever, especially because we were at an all-out
run. Mr. Jarmo had told us that the copper
creatures couldn't move all that fast, but they were
still very dangerous in their own right, being that
their skin was made of some sort of radioactive
acid. It had been sheer luck that had kept us from
getting too close to them during the time we had

already spent in the mines.

The mine shaft suddenly widened into a large cavern, and the ET-7 sat in the middle, its back end partially sunk into the earth, the front of it pointing upward like a rocket ship, its cone-shaped nose directed nearly straight up. Mr. Jarmo scrambled through the open door and into the vessel first, climbing over one seat to get to the other.

"You're both going to have to share that seat!" he said as he took up position in the seat that Calvin had been sitting in earlier. "Climb in and try to strap the safety belt around both of you!"

Although the seat wasn't very big, both Calvin and I managed to fit. I pulled the safety belt around us, and Calvin took it from my hands and snapped it into the buckle. It was a tight fit, but we were secure.

A movement out of the corner of my eye caught my attention, and I turned to look out the door, just in time to see the copper creature emerging into the cavern from the mine shaft. Seeing the beast was both fascinating and horrifying. He was so strange looking, so bizarre. It was almost like seeing a creature from the movies that had jumped down from the screen.

But I knew better. Mr. Jarmo had explained very clearly how dangerous the copper creatures were. I still had many, many questions, but right now, my concern was closing the door, so the giant orange thing couldn't get at us.

Meanwhile, Mr. Jarmo was flipping switches and dials, pressing buttons and adjusting instruments. The door slid closed, and the ET-7's motor roared to life. Then, I could feel us going backward, back into the tunnel that Calvin and I had created.

"We can't go up," Mr. Jarmo said, "because the nose cone isn't touching anything. If we go back into the tunnel, I'll be able to turn the nose cone, and we can level out and go forward."

"Is that how we'll get back to the surface?" I asked.

Mr. Jarmo nodded. "Yes," he replied, "although I've never had the ET-7 above ground before, because I didn't want anyone to discover it. But this is an emergency, and I need to get both of you out of the mine shafts and on your way home."

"I like *that* idea," Calvin said. "What I wouldn't give to be in daylight right now."

The ET-7 continued backing into the earth, but because there were no windows, I had no way to gauge how much progress we were making.

Suddenly, the ET-7 was brought to a jolting halt. The engine abruptly ceased with a violent coughing fit.

I looked at Mr. Jarmo's face and his expression of horror and disbelief.

"No, no, no!" he shouted. *"This can't be happening! This simply can't be happening!"*

26

The panic and alarm in Mr. Jarmo's voice caused a wave of terror to sweep over me, turning my skin to ice. It's not often that I see grown adults so frightened, and that fact alone scared me.

Something really must be wrong, I thought. *Grown-ups don't get scared that easily.*

Mr. Jarmo pressed a button on the panel in front of him. The motor chugged a few times, but it didn't start.

"Come on, come on," he urged as if the ET-7 could hear him and respond. I remember my mom saying those same words when she was trying to get her car started last winter. It was a really frigid morning, and the car engine was so cold that it would barely turn over. Mom had muttered the words, "Come on" five or six times. It must have worked, because after a few more chugs and sputters, the car started.

I wasn't sure if we were going to be so lucky with the ET-7.

"What's wrong?" Calvin asked.

"I don't know," Mr. Jarmo said. "But the main generator that helps power the motor seems to have failed."

Sweat had formed on his face, creating a thin, shiny sheen. He looked worried and concerned as he struggled to get the ET-7 started.

Finally, the engine roared to life once again, and Mr. Jarmo let out a huge sigh of relief. The vehicle shook and trembled, and then we continued going backward, down into the tunnel Calvin and I had created.

I suddenly realized the crazy situation we were in. Earlier in the morning, Calvin and I headed out on our bicycles just to do some exploring and have some fun. Never in my wildest imagination could I have ever thought that we'd be inside an elaborate, earth-dwelling contraption, trying to get away from creatures we never knew existed.

The ET-7 stopped. Mr. Jarmo made some adjustments to the panel in front of him.

"What are you doing now?" I asked.

"I'm turning the drill cone," he replied as he grasped the long, metal control lever next to his seat. "We'll bore into the earth at another angle and then make our way to the surface."

"Does that radar screen show you which direction to go?" Calvin asked.

Mr. Jarmo nodded. "Yes," he replied. "It's a computer navigational system, and it shows a map of the mines and displays which direction we are headed in."

We began moving forward. The ET-7 shook

and rocked as the spinning drill cone at the front of the craft chewed through the earth. Once again, I was fascinated to think that we were aboard a vehicle that was drilling a hole in the ground.

Gradually, I could feel the vessel leveling out. I looked at the computer screen on the panel before us, watching the blinking red dot.

"That's us, right there," Mr. Jarmo said, pointing to the screen. Then, he motioned a little farther up with his finger. "And that's the Earth's surface, right there," he said.

"How come we're not headed up?" I asked.

"We need to make our way around some of the mines and caverns," Mr. Jarmo explained. "The ET-7 can't go through larger caverns, because the nose cone needs substance to chew through. Think of the cone as an enormous drill that pulls itself deeper and deeper. That's how the ET-7 works."

"But if it's the cone that pulls the craft through the earth, how is it that it can go backward?" I asked.

"I built a series of rotating, grinding blades at

the back, just for that purpose," Mr. Jarmo replied. "It took me a long time to get them to work properly, but the blades in back rotate in reverse and allow the ET-7 to retrace its path through the tunnel it's just created for itself."

"And what happens when we get to the surface?" Calvin asked.

"I'll bring us out of the ground far enough to get the door open for you two to get out," Mr. Jarmo replied. "Then, you both can go home."

"But what about you?" I asked.

Mr. Jarmo looked at me. "My work is almost done. I am nearly finished sealing the mine shafts and the other tunnels I've created. And now that you've found my keys, I can lock the doors I've built. Hopefully, that will keep the copper creatures from coming out and making their way to the surface.

"One good thing," he continued, "is that the copper creatures don't like the sunlight. I think it's because of living in the ground, in the dark, for such a long, long time."

"But what if there are copper creatures still in the mines when you seal them up?" Calvin asked. "Won't they be able to climb to the surface and get out at night?"

Mr. Jarmo looked away, and I got an uneasy feeling.

"We'll have to hope that doesn't happen," he said quietly.

I didn't like the sound of that. To me, it sounded like there might be more trouble on the way, and I didn't like that thought at all.

27

None of us spoke for what seemed like a long time. Our eyes were glued to the blinking red dot on the screen. The ET-7 continued to chew through the earth as we slowly made our way toward the surface and to freedom. Our ascent upward was slow and gradual, but we were making progress. It wouldn't be long before we would emerge from the vessel, and I couldn't wait to be standing in daylight once again, breathing in fresh air.

Filled with suspense, Calvin and I continued watching the blinking red dot as it continued to move closer and closer toward the line at the top of the screen that represented the surface. In minutes, our ordeal would be over. We would be safe.

Suddenly, the ET-7 shook violently and lurched to the left, then to the right. We stopped. The engine halted. The lights flickered, then went out.

"I'm afraid to ask," I said, "but what's happened?"

In the darkness, Mr. Jarmo spoke. "I'm not sure," he said. "The ET-7 has never completely lost power before. I'm sure it has something to do with the generator acting up."

Crammed next to me in the seat, Calvin wriggled and squirmed. Then, a tiny beam of light appeared. He had dug into his pocket and pulled out his flashlight.

"I sure am glad you brought that thing," I said.

"Me, too," Calvin replied.

"Shine that over here for just a second," Mr. Jarmo said. "There's an emergency lighting panel just above my head."

Calvin swept the beam over and up. In the gloom, I could see the dark silhouette of Mr. Jarmo as he reached up with his right arm and flipped a switch. Pale white lights lit up the interior of the ET-7, and I felt a wave of relief. While I wasn't sure what had happened or what was going to happen, there was something comforting about being able to see. Darkness just seemed to be so mysterious, so full of the unknown, so cruel and dangerous.

"I'm not sure what happened," Mr. Jarmo said. "But we're very close to the surface, and it looks like we were crisscrossing through a mine shaft when we lost power. We should be able to climb out the door. If I'm right, we'll be able to follow the shaft the rest of the way to the surface."

"I hope you're right," Calvin said. "We've been gone a long time. Mom is probably back from the store, and she's going to be wondering where we are."

"I was just thinking the same thing," I said. "I'll sure be glad when this is all over."

Mr. Jarmo unsnapped his safety belt and stood. He moved toward the door.

"Since there's no power," he said, "I'll have to open the door by unbolting the framework around it."

He knelt down, reached beneath the seat where Calvin and I were sitting, and opened a small, door-like panel that stored a small toolbox. Opening it, he pulled out a wrench and began working at one of the bolts around the door.

"That should do it," he said as he unscrewed the last of them. Then, he gave the door a forceful shove, and it fell away, hitting the rock floor of the mine shaft with a loud clang.

"Good news," Mr. Jarmo said. "I was right. We're in the middle of a mine shaft, and I know this one well. We're near the surface, and we can follow it to the entrance on the side of a hill."

He reached into the toolbox again and pulled out a large flashlight. Switching it on, he aimed the bright beam out the door, illuminating the rock walls and the two metal rail tracks that snaked through the shaft.

Calvin unsnapped the seat belt, and we both scrambled from our seats. I couldn't wait to get out of the mines, to be back on the surface of the Earth. It seemed as if we had been in darkness for days, trudging through the mines beneath Calumet.

Mr. Jarmo slipped out the door, then grabbed my hand and helped me out. Calvin scrambled out on his own, and the three of us stood next to the huge, earth-drilling vehicle that Mr. Jarmo had built. He shined the light over the craft, inspecting it.

"Well, I suppose I can find out what's wrong after we get you two out of here," he said, sweeping the flashlight beam down the shaft. "That's the important thing right now. We're not far. Let's go."

Suddenly, there was a noise from behind us, in the shaft. To my horror, when I turned around, I saw an enormous, glowing creature coming toward us!

28

"Quickly!" Mr. Jarmo said. "We can move faster than the creature, and we're not far from the surface entrance to the mine shaft! Let's go!"

Mr. Jarmo aimed the flashlight down the mine shaft, and the three of us started running. For an old guy, he was able to gallop along pretty well. Actually, I was surprised at how fast he could run.

"You're sure the creature won't follow us out of the mine shaft?" I panted as we ran.

"It's possible," he replied, "but as far as I know, the creatures have never left the safety of the mine shafts. Once we make it out, we'll be safe."

That was great news, and once again I thought how great it was going to feel when we got out of the mine.

"I've got to slow down," Mr. Jarmo said. "I can't keep up this pace any longer."

He slowed to a brisk walk, as did Calvin and I. Then, I shot a glance over my shoulder, relieved to see only darkness and not the hideous orange copper creature, glad to know that they weren't anywhere near as fast as we were.

"How much farther?" Calvin asked.

"I'm not sure," Mr. Jarmo replied. "But according to the computer navigation system, the ET-7 stalled out very close to the surface. We can't be far."

"There!" I blurted out as I saw a gleam of light ahead of us that was, unmistakably, daylight. It was just a small sliver, but it was enough to know that our trek through the mine shaft was nearly

over. Soon, we would be safely outside—in the daylight—where the copper creatures wouldn't be able to get to us.

Like many other entrances to the mines, the opening to the shaft was sealed off. Long ago, Mr. Jarmo and his fellow workers had nailed boards and affixed metal pipes over the entrance. We would have to remove them to get out, and it was going to take some time.

"Let's get to work," Mr. Jarmo said. "Some of these slats are old and should break away. If we can just get a few of the boards off and bend some of the bars, we'll be able to get outside."

The three of us began pulling and pushing at the old wooden slats and metal bars, but it was slow going. Whoever had sealed off the mine shaft didn't want anyone to get in . . . or anything to get out.

That, unfortunately, was going to be our undoing. It was taking a long time to break away the slats and work the bars loose, and it was time we no longer had.

Behind us, the copper creature was making his deadly approach, and we had succeeded in making only a small opening, which wasn't yet big enough for any one of us to get through.

"Hurry!" Mr. Jarmo said. *"We're almost there!"*

We continued working, pulling and pushing the wooden slats and bars, trying to break them away.

All the while, the hulking copper creature was getting closer, and closer, and closer . . . .

29

The sight of the approaching beast gave the three of us renewed strength. We began lashing out, kicking at the slats until more began to break away. I was able to work two metal pipes loose and push them aside.

Meanwhile, the copper creature was getting closer and closer.

"There!" Mr. Jarmo said as several slats fell away. He grabbed Calvin by the shoulders and

shoved him through the ragged hole we had created. Calvin got hung up for a moment as some of the broken wood slats caught his clothing, but he managed to wiggle through.

"*Go!*" Mr. Jarmo said to me, and I didn't waste any time. I knelt down and scrambled through the hole. Like Calvin, I got stuck on some of the sharp pieces of wood and pieces of metal, but my brother came to my aid, grabbing my arms and pulling me into the bright daylight.

Mr. Jarmo was next, but he was much bigger than we were and was having a difficult time.

Behind him, in the shaft, the enormous copper creature was getting closer.

"*Grab his hand!*" I shouted to Calvin. "*We've got to pull him through!*"

We each grasped one of his wrists and pulled with all the strength we had. It took a moment, but we were able to finally succeed in pulling him out. Mr. Jarmo collapsed in a heap, gasping on the ground just outside the entrance, at the base of a large, sloping, barren hill.

In the mine, on the other side of the boarded-up entrance, the copper creature stood, frozen like a statue. It was obvious that he wasn't going to come any closer, even if he could break through what remained of the wood slats and metal bars that still covered most of the entrance. Mr. Jarmo had been right: the creature did not like even the small amount of daylight that was trickling into the shaft.

After a moment, the creature backed away. We watched him through the broken slats covering the entrance, until the creature finally turned and vanished back into the darkness of the mine shaft.

It felt so good to finally be out of the mines. I was squinting, because my eyes had not yet adjusted to the daylight, but my vision was getting better and better with every passing second.

I looked around. We were in, most obviously, an abandoned mining area. On one side, the hill rose above us, containing the skeletal remains of what once had been a mining operation. On the other side of us, the ground leveled out. There were several old buildings with their doors and windows boarded up. Some of them appeared to be falling in on themselves. It occurred to me that we really had no idea where we were, and I also had no idea how we would find our bicycles.

Still, I wasn't all that concerned. I was just glad to be out of the mines and away from those horrible copper creatures lurking in the mines beneath the surface.

"Now what?" Calvin asked.

"Now, I have a mission to finish," Mr. Jarmo said as he held up his wad of keys. "I've got to lock the doors and seal in the copper creatures once and for all. You two be on your way. I have a lot of work to do, and I'm afraid I can't help you any more."

"Don't worry about us," I said. "We'll find our way home. I'm more worried about you."

Mr. Jarmo shook his head. "No need to worry about me," he said. "I've been in and out of these mines thousands of times since they were shut down years ago. They've become my second home.

I've always been able to stay one step ahead of the creatures. I'll be fine."

Calvin and I said good-bye to Mr. Jarmo. He waved at us as we walked off. It was the last time we ever saw him. To this day, I wonder if he succeeded in his mission. I wonder if the copper creatures are gone for good or whether they wander the mine shafts beneath Calumet. Mr. Jarmo said the creatures don't like daylight, but that wouldn't stop them from coming out at night.

Yes, I still wonder about that, and sometimes, I still have nightmares.

To get out of the abandoned mining property, we had to crawl under a wire fence. Then, we followed a dirt road until it met a paved highway, where we instantly recognized where we were. We followed the road until, to our shock and horror, we saw something we never expected to see: in the distance was a flash of orange in the ditch.

And it was moving.

Mr. Jarmo had been wrong. The copper

creatures had come out into the daylight, after all . . . and if that was the case, it was going to spell big trouble for us, and everyone in Calumet.

30

Calvin and I stopped walking and froze, but it didn't take long to realize that what we were looking at wasn't a copper creature. It was simply a road worker, picking up trash along the shoulder of the highway. He was wearing an orange vest that, at first glance, made it look like he was one of those horrible copper creatures.

"I thought he was a copper creature!" Calvin said.

"I did, too," I said.

Just then, the worker looked up and saw us. He waved, and we waved back.

Then, I laughed. Calvin laughed, too.

"It feels good to laugh," I said. "We haven't had anything to laugh about all day."

We continued walking and finally came to the path that we followed earlier in the day on our bikes: the same path that led us to the place where we'd fallen into the mine.

We found our bicycles without any trouble, and we were careful not to go anywhere near the mine shaft we'd fallen into. We didn't want to go through that again!

Then, we set out for home . . . but two strange things happened before we got there.

On the shoulder of the road, we came across a broken down vehicle. A man was kneeling next to it, and as we approached, we realized he was changing a tire. He saw us coming and waved. We coasted up alongside the car and stopped.

"Flat tire?" Calvin asked.

The man nodded. "Yeah," he replied. "I think I ran over a nail or something."

The man looked familiar. He had black hair pulled back into a long ponytail, along with a black goatee. But the strangest part were his sunglasses. They appeared to have eyeballs that changed colors! I thought I recognized the man from somewhere, but I couldn't be sure. There was something very familiar about him, but I couldn't put my finger on just what it was.

"Do you need some help?" I asked.

"No, thanks," the man replied. "I think I can handle it. I'm glad I left early. I'm headed for a writer's conference over in Wisconsin."

"Is that what you do?" Calvin asked. "Write books?"

"Yes," the man replied.

"What kind of books?" I asked.

"Oh, you know," the man said as he lowered the jack and began packing up his tools. "Scary books. Books about strange happenings."

"We just had something strange happen to

us," Calvin said, and without waiting for the man to reply, my brother rattled off our entire ordeal. The man listened intently, and he seemed very interested in what Calvin was saying.

By the time my brother was finished, the man had packed up all of his tools and put them in the trunk of his car. He looked at Calvin, then at me.

"Did this really happen to you guys?" he asked. Then, he pointed to the ground. "Are there really copper creatures in the mines beneath Calumet?"

Calvin and I nodded.

"Yes," I replied. "Every word of what my brother said is true."

"I'd like to use that idea for a book, if you don't mind," the man said. "I'll bet I could write a pretty creepy story about copper creatures."

"That would be great!" I said. "Will you use our names?"

The man shook his head. "My books are works of fiction, and that includes the characters. I'll change it around a little bit, but I'll base the story on exactly what you've told me. Sound cool?"

Did it ever! Not only did this man believe us, but he was going to write a book about our horrifying ordeal!

The man got into his car and drove away.

"That's cool!" Calvin exclaimed. "He's going to write a book about us!"

I shook my head. "Not us," I said. "But it will be cool to have a published story about what happened to us, even if he does change some of the facts."

Calvin and I continued on our bikes, riding along the shoulder of the road, heading toward home. Oddly enough, we came across another broken down car. A man and a woman were standing next to it, and the woman was talking on a phone.

We rode up to the car and stopped.

"What's the matter?" I asked the man.

He shook his head. "I don't know," he replied. "We were driving along, and all of a sudden, the car lost power. Now, it won't start. My sister, Sandy, is calling for a tow truck."

"Bummer," Calvin said.

"You're telling me," the man said, rolling his eyes. "We're headed for Mackinac Island for a family reunion, and the last thing we needed was for our car to break down."

Sandy pulled the phone from her ear and slipped it into her purse. "The tow truck will be here soon, Tim," she said to her brother. Then, she looked at us and smiled. "Hello," she said.

"Hi," Calvin and I each said.

"It looks like we're going to be stuck in Calumet for a while," Sandy said. "At least until they can get our car fixed."

"At least you don't have to worry about copper creatures," Calvin said, and he immediately went into the story once again. Tim and Sandy listened just as intently as the other man had. When Calvin finished, Tim and Sandy looked at each other.

"We had a bizarre thing happen to us, years ago, on Mackinac Island," Tim said. He looked at his sister. "Remember, Sandy?"

"How could I ever forget?" Sandy replied. "Even today, years later, it seems like a nightmare."

"What happened to you guys?" I asked.

"Something crazy," Sandy replied, shaking her head. She looked at Calvin and me. "You'd never believe it."

"I'd believe a lot right now," I said. "Especially after what we just went through."

"Well," Tim said. "We have some time before the wrecker arrives. Would you like us to tell you about it?"

"Yeah!" Calvin said. "What happened to you guys?"

"I'll start," Sandy said. "It all began as a normal day on Mackinac Island."

Calvin and I listened, totally enthralled and amazed at what had happened to Sandy and Tim on Mackinac Island all those years ago . . . .

Where the spellbinding series began!

Johnathan Rand's

MICHIGAN CHILLERS

#1 Mayhem on Mackinac Island

Continue on to read the first few chapters for FREE!

My name is Sandy, and I'm twelve. Sandra Jean
Johnson, if you're really mad at me. But usually
everybody calls me Sandy, except my brother Tim. He
calls me a lot of other dumb names . . . names that he
makes up, mostly. Silly names . . . like *Sandy-Pandy*
and *Sandra Jean, the Queen of Mean*. Which isn't fair,
because I'm not mean. And he calls me *Munchkin*. I
hate that one the worst. It even *sounds* bad.

Munchkin.

I'm a year older than he is, but I'm about an inch
shorter. Just because of that, he calls me Munchkin.

I hate being called that.

I have sandy-blonde hair that fits my name perfectly. It's just past my shoulders.

Once I got it cut real short, but I didn't like it. Now I wear it long, sometimes in a pony-tail or a French braid. Tim has hair a little darker than mine, only his is a lot shorter.

Of all the seasons, I like summer the best. We live in Birmingham, Michigan, but we spend the whole summer on Mackinac Island. It's about a five hour drive from our house in Birmingham.

Mackinac Island is an island in Lake Huron, which is one of the Great Lakes. Actually, in my opinion, it's bigger than a Great Lake. It's HUGE! Much bigger than any lake I've ever seen. It's so blue and beautiful that sometimes I never want to leave. There are lots of trees on the island, and I meet lots of cool new friends every summer. Every summer we have a blast.

Except for *this* summer.

This summer turned into a horrible nightmare—worse than I could have ever imagined.

But first, I guess I have to tell you about what

went on *last* summer. That's when something really weird happened.

Tim and I were at our Uncle Jerry's house . . . that's the house we stay at on Mackinac Island. Mom and dad and Tim and I stay with Uncle Jerry and Aunt Ruth. We stay from June all the way till school starts. It's so much fun! Aunt Ruth and Uncle Jerry are really nice. Their house is really big and pretty and it's right near the water. They have a dock that extends way out over the lake. There's even a diving board there! We swim a lot and go for boat rides.

I asked Dad one day if I could ride my bike all the way around the paved footpath that goes around the island. It's a long way . . . like eight miles or something.

"Okay," Dad told me. "But Tim has to go with you."

"Great," I whispered, rolling my eyes. I did NOT want Tim to go with me!

Tim was in his bedroom playing his Game Boy, but he heard us talking. "Hey, that sounds like fun!" he yelled. He ran into the living room where I was. "Let's go Munchkin!" he said.

Terrific.

"Come on, slow poke!" he said, running out the door. He already had his helmet on!

I wish I could do some things all by myself once in a while.

But something was about to happen on the bike trip that made me glad that we were together.

REALLY glad.

2

My bike is red. Tim's is blue. They're mountain bikes
. . . we each got one for Christmas that year. Before
that, we rented bikes from a store on the island.

Anyway, we peddled through downtown. I
LOVE downtown Mackinac Island! They don't allow
cars on the island—anywhere! We can ride our bikes in
the middle of the street if we want to.

But—

You have to watch out! There are lots of other
people on bikes and even more people walking . . . but
the thing you really have to watch out for is the horses!

On Mackinac Island, horses are used to pull carriages and wagons! Since there are no cars, horses pull buggies around the island. The buggies and carriages carry everything from luggage to supplies to people. You can even go for a tour on a horse drawn carriage if you want.

But the best thing about downtown is the delicious aroma of sweet, tantalizing fudge! It's everywhere—drifting out from the stores, through open doors and windows—yum! I could eat fudge all day.

You probably could, too, if you stayed on Mackinac Island all summer.

"Watch out!" I suddenly yelled at Tim. He wasn't watching where he was going and he almost ran into a man pushing a cart! Tim swerved just in time. That was a close one.

We rode through town and continued on the paved blacktop path that winds all around the island. It's a fun ride. You can see boats on the water, and even the Michigan mainland in the distance. And seagulls! There are lots of seagulls whirling above and sitting near the shore.

When we were about halfway around the island,

Tim stopped. "I'm tired," he said. "I need to rest." He hopped off and laid his bike against a tree. He took his helmet off and set it on his bike seat.

For the first time in my life, I think I actually agreed with him. I was tired, too.

I hopped off my bike and walked down to the water where Tim was. He was skipping rocks.

I picked up a nice flat rock and let it fly. It skipped fifteen times!

"Showoff!" Tim said. But he was just jealous. He knew he couldn't skip a rock fifteen times if he tried! I felt proud.

Suddenly, he turned and pointed. "Look at that!" he said.

I turned and I couldn't believe what I saw. I mean . . . I just couldn't! I had to get closer and get a better look.

And THAT'S what got us into trouble.

3

It was a man! A very small man, sitting in a great big tree. He had long gray hair that flowed over his shoulders and a long gray beard. And a tall, funny hat that was cone-shaped. The hat had silver and gold stars all over it. He was wearing a long white robe. Boy! Did he look out of place on Mackinac Island, not to mention the fact that he was sitting in a tree! He looked like he was a magician or something.

The tree he was sitting in was really old looking. It had a lot of long, black spiny branches, like thin fingers, but no leaves. I was sure that the tree was dead.

"Hello!" Tim shouted. He said it so loud and unexpectedly that I jumped. I hate it when he does that.

The sound must have scared the man because all of a sudden he disappeared! I caught a flash of his white robe, and it looked like he just ran along the branch and into the tree!

Tim wanted to find out where he went. "Come on, Munchkin!" he said, running past our bikes and into the woods.

"Quit calling me Munchkin!" I scolded. But I followed him anyway.

The forest on the other side of the paved footpath was really thick. There was no trail so I had to use my arms to pull branches and limbs out of my way. It was so thick that it was hard to walk. Trees grew close together and there were vines and small branches everywhere.

I accidentally walked into a spider web and the thin gooey string stuck to my face. Pitooey! I hate spiders. I wiped the sticky web away with my hands and continued after Tim.

But there was something that was very strange.

We walked and walked, but we couldn't find the

little old man! It was like he just disappeared completely. Weird.

Tim stopped beneath the old tree, looking up and around. "I wonder where he went," he said, gazing up into the branches. I stopped walking too.

I looked up, peering through the dense limbs above, but I didn't see any sign of the man. I was really hoping I would be the first to see the tiny man again. Tim is always discovering new things first, but I wanted to be first this time.

The forest was very quiet. On Mackinac Island you obviously don't hear any cars, because there aren't any. Once in a while you hear a plane overhead. But all we could hear in the forest were birds. Birds and crickets.

"He couldn't just disappear into thin air," I said.

"Maybe he disappeared into fat air," Tim said, making fun of me.

"There's no such thing as fat air!" I said. But then again, maybe there was. I didn't know for sure.

We stared up into the trees for a few more seconds, but we didn't see any sign of the man with the white robe and funny hat.

"Let's go back," Tim said finally, taking one last look up into the trees. I followed his gaze and we squinted up into the sky.

No funny old man. He had disappeared.

I turned and started to walk back to the footpath. My feet crunched on sticks and branches.

"Aaahhhhhhgggghh!!" someone screamed in terror, and I recognized the voice instantly.

That someone was Tim!

4

I stopped and spun around. Tim was staring at his feet. He was trying to walk, but he couldn't.

His feet were trapped in quicksand!

It was all the way up and over his ankles. Tim grabbed a branch and tried to pull himself out. He freed one foot but the other one kept getting sucked farther into the ground!

"Help me Munchkin!" he yelled. I would have been mad at him for calling me Munchkin, but I was too scared. Tim was in trouble, and I needed to help.

I walked toward him, watching the ground

carefully. I didn't want to step into quicksand too!

I couldn't get real close to him because there was quicksand all around him. Dark, syrup-like mud was everywhere.

"Hurry!" Tim said. He was sinking faster, and the brown goo was almost up to his knee. He held his other leg up in the air as far as he could so it wouldn't get stuck again. If he wasn't in so much danger he would've looked very funny!

I searched around and found a long stick.

"Grab this!" I hollered, holding it out.

Tim grabbed it and I pulled with all my might. I'm not very big, but I'm really pretty strong. I think I'm even stronger than Tim.

I pulled and pulled like I never had before. I felt like I was in a game of tug-o-war . . . a *dangerous* game of tug-o-war . . . and if I didn't win, we were really going to be in trouble.

But I wasn't going to lose. I was sure of it. I kept pulling harder and harder on the branch.

"Hang on tight!" I told Tim. "Whatever you do, don't let go!"

Finally Tim's foot came free. He tumbled

forward and I lost my balance, falling back. Tim landed on top of me.

"Get off me, you goof," I told him. But I really was glad that he was okay.

"That was close, Munch," he said.

Munch. I think that's worse than being called Munchkin.

He stood up, looking at his leg. His sneaker and the leg of his pants were covered with brown gunk all the way up to his knee.

"Mom's gonna freak out," he said. But I know he was really glad that he got out of the quicksand. If he had been stuck for just a few more seconds, there's no telling what would have happened.

But all of this happened last summer.

What happened this summer was worse.

FAR worse.

5

Tim and I were riding our bikes around town, but it started raining so we hung out downtown for awhile. I went into the Island Bookstore and Tim went into the toy store. We both went into a couple of fudge shops, and I bought a big chunk of fudge called 'Moose Tracks'. Yum!

Finally the rain stopped and we got on our bikes again. We rode by the marina, and past the big white fort on the hill. The Governor of Michigan even has a summer home on Mackinac Island, and we rode past it, too.

There were a lot of people walking on the path, but the farther we got from town, the less people there were. Soon we didn't see anyone anymore.

By this time we had pretty much forgotten all about the old man and the tree and the quicksand.

So when I was riding past the spot where we had spotted the old man last year, I couldn't believe my eyes!

"Tim, look!" I shouted. Tim was in front of me riding his blue bike. He stopped and turned to see where I was pointing.

It was the same strange old man with the funny hat!

He was sitting in the same old tree in the same place where he had been last year. Same long, gray hair and beard. Same weird looking pointy hat with gold and silver stars. He wasn't more than fifty feet away from us.

"Hey!" Tim shouted. Sometimes when Tim says 'hey' what he really means is 'hello.'

I was sure the old man was going to run away, just like he did last year.

But he didn't.

In fact, the old man did just the opposite. He waved at us, urging us to come closer.

"Come on," Tim said, hopping off his bike.

"No, Tim," I said. "Let's stay here." But actually, I wanted to go see for myself, too.

"Oh, come on Munchkin," he whined.

"Remember what happened last year," I reminded him.

"Don't worry, I'll watch out," he replied, referring to the quicksand.

I reluctantly followed him into the woods and looked up. To my surprise, the old man was still in the tree, smiling, still waving at us to come forward. I was walking slow, keeping a close watch on the ground. I sure didn't want to step in any quicksand!

When we got close to the tree we stopped, and guess what?

The old man had disappeared again!

So strange.

"Where in the world did he go?" Tim asked, staring up into the branches. I looked up into the tree, too . . . but I kept glancing down at the ground, expecting to see quicksand. I was relieved when I didn't see any.

"This is just like last year," I whispered. "He disappeared last year, too."

"Well, I'm *going* to go find him," Tim stated seriously. "People just don't *disappear*." He walked toward the trunk of the huge, dead tree and looked up.

"What are you *doing?!?*" I asked him. But I already knew.

Tim was going to climb the tree!

"No, Tim!" I told him. "I don't think it's a good idea."

And it wasn't a good idea. It wasn't a good idea at all, as we were about to find out.

ABOUT THE AUTHOR

Johnathan Rand has been called 'one of the most prolific authors of the century.' He has authored more than 75 books since the year 2000, with well over 4 million copies in print. His series include the incredibly popular **AMERICAN CHILLERS, MICHIGAN CHILLERS, FREDDIE FERNORTNER, FEARLESS FIRST GRADER,** and **THE ADVENTURE CLUB.** He's also co-authored a novel for teens (with Christopher Knight) entitled **PANDEMIA**. When not traveling, Rand lives in northern Michigan with his wife and three dogs. He is also the only author in the world to have a store that sells only his works: **CHILLERMANIA!** is located in Indian River, Michigan and is open year round. Johnathan Rand is not always at the store, but he has been known to drop by frequently. Find out more at:

www.americanchillers.com

Johnathan Rand travels internationally for school visits and book signings! For booking information, call:

1 (231) 238-0338!

Dont Miss:

Join the official

AMERICAN CHILLERS

FAN CLUB!

Visit www.americanchillers.com for details!

Also by Johnathan Rand:

GHOST IN THE GRAVEYARD

All AudioCraft books are proudly printed, bound, and manufactured in the United States of America, utilizing American resources, labor, and materials.

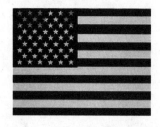

USA